The huge fist of th[illegible]
warning, into his fa[illegible]
More intense than the pain was the feeling of consuming rage. He was on his feet again with a catlike agility, his own fists pounding into the bloated belly of the guard. Again he fell, this time under a rain of blows from behind. He was sufficiently in control of himself to roll into a ball, protecting his face with his arms from the heavy boots. It seemed far too long a time before he lost consciousness.

Also by A. Bertram Chandler in Sphere Books:

THE RIM OF SPACE
WHEN THE DREAM DIES
BRING BACK YESTERDAY

Beyond the Galactic Rim

A. BERTRAM CHANDLER

SPHERE BOOKS LIMITED
30-32 Gray's Inn Road, London WC1X 8JL

First published in Great Britain by
Sphere Books Ltd 1982

TRADE
MARK

Set in Baskerville

Printed and bound in Great Britain by
Hunt Barnard Printing Ltd, Aylesbury, Bucks.

Contents

Forbidden Planet

She was a large hunk of ship, was *Sally Ann*, too large and too imposing for the name she bore. She stood proudly in her berth at Port Forlorn, dwarfing cranes and gantries and administration buildings, towering high above *Rimstar* and *Rimbound*, both typical units of the Rim Runners' fleet. Yet, to the trained eye of a spaceman, a relationship between *Sally Ann* and the smaller vessels would have been obvious – all three bore the unmistakable stamp of the Interstellar Transport Commission and all three had come down in the Universe. *Sally Ann*, for all her outward smartness, had come down the furthest; she had been a Beta-class liner, and now she was tramping. *Rimstar* and *Rimbound* had been Epsilon-class tramps and now they were dignified with the name of cargo liners.

Commodore Grimes, astronautical superintendent for Rim Runners, looked out from the window of his office towards the big ship, screwing up his eyes against the steely glare of the westering sun. His hard, pitted face softened momentarily as he said, 'I'm sorry, Captain. We can't use her. She just won't fit into any of our trades.'

'Fletcher, your agent on Van Diemen's Planet, assured me that I should be sure of getting a charter as soon as I got out of here,' said Captain Clavering. 'I've delivered the load of migrants that you were clamouring for; now it's up to you to at least give me profitable employment back to the Centre.'

'You had nothing in writing,' stated Grimes. 'You took Fletcher's word for it. I know Fletcher – he used to be a purser in your old concern, Trans-Galactic Clippers. He's got that typical big ship purser's knack of seeming to promise everything whilst, in reality, promising nothing.' He got to his feet and pointed towards *Rimstar*. 'There's the sort of ship that you and your friends should have bought when you won that lottery. A tramp can always make a living of sorts out on the Rim – one of our captains came into a large sum of salvage money and bought a tramp; he's running the Eastern Circuit on time charter to us ...'

'I heard about him,' admitted Clavering. 'He pulled *Thermopylae* off Eblis. I was in her for a while after she got back to her normal running ... But, Commodore, what Calver's doing has nothing to do with *my* problems. Surely there must be some passenger traffic on the Rim. Fletcher told me ...'

'Fletcher would tell you anything,' snapped Grimes. 'If you've seen one Rim World you've seen them all. Why should anybody want to proceed from Lorn to Faraway, or from Ultimo to Thule? The handful of people who must travel for business reasons we can carry in our own ships – they're all fitted with accommodation for twelve passengers, and it's rarely used.

'In any case, why this desire on your part to run the Rim? We have a saying, you know – a man who comes out to the Rim to make his living would go to Hell for a pastime.'

'Because,' said Clavering bitterly, 'I thought it was the only part of the Galaxy where a tramp passenger ship could make a living. It seems that I was mistaken.'

Grimes got to his feet, held out his hand to the younger man in a gesture of dismissal. He said, 'I'm sorry, Captain, I mean it. I hate to see a good spaceman with a large white elephant hanging around his neck. If I hear of any profitable employment at all, I'll let you know – but I can't hold out much hope.'

'Thank you,' said Clavering.

He shook hands with Grimes and strode out of the office, walked with a briskness that masked his reluctance to face his shipmates, his fellow shareholders, across the windswept, dusty apron to his ship.

They were waiting for him in *Sally Ann*'s shabby, but still comfortable, lounge. There was Sally Ann Clavering who, in addition to being his wife, combined the functions of Purser and Catering Officer. There was Taubman, chief and only Reaction Drive Engineer, and Rokovsky, who was in charge of the Interstellar Drive. There was Larwood, Chief Officer, and Mary Larwood, the biochemist. The few remaining officers were not shareholders and were not present.

Clavering maintained his stiffness as he entered the lounge, by his bearing counteracting the shabbiness of his uniform. His lean face, under the greying hair, was expressionless.

'So they have nothing for us,' stated Sally Ann flatly.

'They have nothing for us,' agreed Clavering tonelessly, watching disappointment momentarily soften the fine lines of his wife's face, watching it succeeded by a combination of hope – surely a hopeless hope – and determination.

'We'd have been better off,' growled burly, black-bearded Rokovsky, 'if we'd never won that blasted lottery. What do we do now? Sell the ship for scrap, hoping that she'll bring enough to pay our passages back to civilisation? Or do we lay her up and get jobs with Rim Runners?'

'It was a gamble,' said Larwood, 'and it just didn't come off. But we were all in it.' *And I'll gamble again*, said the expression on his dark, reckless face. *And I*, declared the mobile features of his wife.

'At least,' pointed out the slight, heavily bespectacled

Taubman, 'we have reaction mass enough to take us up and clear of the planet, and the Pile's good for a few years yet.'

'And where do we go from here?' demanded Rokovsky.

'And what do we use for money to pay the last of the bills?' asked Sally Ann.

'Buy another ticket in the Nine Worlds Lottery,' suggested Larwood.

'What with?' she countered. 'The prizes are big, as we know, but those tickets are expensive. And we have to get back to the Nine Worlds first, anyhow.'

'Damn it all!' exploded Clavering. 'We've got a ship, a good ship. We didn't show the profit that we should have done on that load of migrants, but that doesn't mean that there's no profit to be made elsewhere in the Galaxy. That Psionic radio operator of ours will just have to wake up his dog's brain in aspic and keep a real listening watch for a change. There must be *something* somewhere – a planet newly opened up for colonisation, some world threatened by disaster and a demand for ships for the evacuation ...'

'He says that it's time that he got paid,' stated Sally Ann. 'And so does Sparks.'

'And the second mate,' added Larwood, 'And the quack.'

'What fittings can we sell?' asked Clavering hopelessly. 'What can we do without?'

'Nothing,' replied his wife.

'We could ...' began Clavering, then paused, listening. Faintly at first, then rising in intensity, there was the wailing, urgent note of a siren, loud enough to penetrate the shell plating and the insulation of the ship. Without a word the Captain got to his feet, strode towards the doorway of the axial shaft and the little elevator that would take him up to the control room. Wordlessly, the others followed. This, obviously, was some kind of emergency – and in an emergency the spaceman's conditioned reflexes impel him automatically towards his station.

Clavering and his officers crowded into the little elevator cage, waited impatiently as it bore them upwards to the nose of the ship. They almost ran into the control room, looked out through the big ports.

The sun was down and the sky was already dark save for the pale glow in the west. Falling slowly, winking balefully, were the red stars of the warning rockets that had been fired from the control tower. Scurrying out on to the spaceport apron like huge beetles, the beams of their headlights like questing antennae in the dusty air, were two red painted fire trucks and the ambulance. There was activity around the two Rim Runners' ships, *Rimstar* and *Rimbound,* as their personnel hurried out of the airlock doors and down the ramps.

'There!' cried Larwood, pointing.

Clavering looked up, almost directly overhead, and saw a fitful glare in the sky. There was a ship there, and she was coming down, and the siren and the red rockets and the lifesaving equipment made it obvious that she was in some kind of trouble. There had been, he remembered, a ship due that evening – *Faraway Quest.*

'Switch on the transceiver,' he ordered.

Larwood had anticipated the command. Suddenly there was a fresh voice in the control room – a crisp voice, calm, yet with an underlying note of anxiety.

'Impossible to pull out and clear. Numbers one and two liners gone, number three tube liner starting to melt. Will try to bring her in on the other three – if they hold that long.'

Grimes' voice replied. 'Do your best, Captain.'

'What the hell do you think I am doing? This is my ship, Commodore, and it's the lives of my crew and passengers that are at stake. *Do your best*! What else is there to do?'

'I'm sorry, Captain,' replied Grimes.

'Just keep off the air, will you?' snapped the other. 'I've a job of work to do, and I can't do it if you keep nattering. Just have everything ready in case of a crash, that's all. Over and *out*!'

'Do you think he'll make it?' asked Larwood, of nobody in particular.

'He has to,' said Clavering shortly. *He has to,* he thought. *He'll have to fight her down every inch of the way, anticipating every yaw. The servo-mechanisms in those old Epsilon-class ships were never designed to cope with any real emergency ...*

He found his binoculars, adjusted the polarisation, stared up at the descending ship. He was no engineer, but even to him the irregular pulse of the exhaust looked unhealthy, as did the great gouts of flame that dropped from it, the incandescent, molten ceramic of the liners. He could make out faintly the shape of the vessel above the blinding glare of the back-blast, saw that her captain was maintaining her in an upright position.

The noise of her passage was audible now, drowning the screaming voice of the siren, pulsating as irregularly as the siren had done. At times it was almost the full throated roar of a full powered ship, at times it died to a querulous mutter. If the rockets failed entirely she would fall. Desperately, Clavering willed them not to fail, knew that the others with him were doing the same. If will power could have sustained *Faraway Quest* it would have done – but there is a limit to the weight that even a team of trained teleporteurs can handle, and even a small ship is far in excess of that limit.

Down she dropped, lower and lower, making for the berth midway between *Sally Ann* and the nearer of the two Rim ships. Still she was under control, although beginning to yaw heavily. *He'll make it,* thought Clavering, *he'll make it.* Dimly he was aware of his wife's hand on his arm, gripping it painfully, dimly he was aware of the muttered curses of Rokovsky, the tense whispering of Larwood – 'You're almost home. Stay with it man, stay with it!' – the heavy breathing of Taubman.

With feet only to go, the last of the tubes blew, blinding the watchers. They heard the crash, heard the notes of the siren swell to fill the silence that followed immediately, heard the noise of shouting.

Slowly their vision cleared. Through streaming eyes Clavering stared out from the view port, saw *Faraway Quest* standing there, gleaming in the beams of the searchlights. He thought at first that she had, miraculously, escaped damage – then saw that her vanes had driven deep into the concrete, that her stern was crumpled. An arc flared bluely in the vicinity of her airlock door as the rescue began to burn its way into the ship. Grimes' voice was barking from the speaker of the transceiver, 'Captain! Captain Hall! What casualties have you?'

The voice that replied was faint and unutterably weary. 'I . . . I don't know yet. No reply from the reaction drive room. The engineers . . .'

'I can guess,' said Taubman heavily.

'We all can,' said Clavering. 'It's an ill wind. If anybody had been killed in *Faraway Quest* I shouldn't be feeling so happy about it, but even those in the reaction drive room escaped with only a bad shaking.'

Sally Ann laid down her pen, looked up from the store sheet that she was checking. As she looked at her husband's face the frown lifted from her own. 'Tell!' she ordered. 'What are you so cheerful about?'

'Grimes sent for me,' said Clavering.

'I know,' she said. 'What did he want you for?'

'I'm coming to that. *Faraway Quest* is, as you know, a converted Epsilon-class tramp. She is – or was – a survey ship of sorts, which means that cargo space had been for the accommodation of personnel. She had a full load of scientists when she crashed here – she was on her way to Eblis to carry out a proper exploration ...'

'Eblis,' said his wife. 'That's the world that *Thermopylae* was almost lost on ...'

'That's right. Anyhow, there's this expedition fitted out at great expense and no ship to carry it. *Faraway Quest* can be made space-worthy again, but it'll not be done in five minutes. Meanwhile, here at Port Forlorn, is one large vessel – complete with ample accommodation and storage space – a large vessel, furthermore, that's just pining for a charter ...'

'You mean that they want us?' she demanded.

'Who else?' he countered. 'Meanwhile, call a general meeting of the shareholders – they're apt to sulk, Rokovsky especially, if anything is done without their being consulted.'

'I,' she said, 'will do just that.'

'Also,' he told her, 'you can tell the hired help that they're getting paid.'

He left her to make the arrangements, went into the lounge, sat in his usual chair. Larwood came in, his wife with him. They smiled at the captain, knowing from his expression that he had good news for them. Rokovsky, morose as always, joined them, and the only slightly less gloomy Taubman. Lastly, Sally Ann entered briskly, carrying a large folder of papers.

She remained standing, said, 'The Chairman of the Board of Directors will now address you.' She sat down as Clavering got to his feet.

Briefly, yet omitting nothing, Clavering told them of his meeting with Grimes. He said that *Sally Ann* would be on hire for a minimum period of six months, and that during this time all expenses – wages, propellant, supplies – would be paid by Rim Runners.

'And what,' asked Larwood, 'about insurance? Lloyd's

have a list of proscribed planets and Eblis is on the list. We can land – but it means ruinous premiums if we do. Or are we just hanging off in orbit and sending the scientists down in the boats?'

'We are landing,' said Clavering. 'Grimes assures me that there is a plateau in the northern hemisphere that's quite safe. Rim Runners are looking after our insurance in any case.'

'And what sort of planet is this Eblis?' demanded Rokovsky.

'It's just what its name implies,' replied Clavering. 'It's in the throes of perpetual vulcanism. The atmosphere's a fine, rich mixture of carbon dioxide, sulphur dioxide and a few more noxious gases. The seas are practically undiluted acid. The electrical storms are so spectacular as to be clearly visible from over a thousand miles out in Space ...'

'Any life?' asked Mary Larwood.

'That's one of the things the expedition hopes to find out,' Clavering told her.

'We shall be risking the ship,' grumbled Rokovsky.

'She'll be well covered,' Clavering assured him.

'And our lives,' continued the engineer.

'We're spacemen,' said Larwood, 'and we risk our lives every time that we lift from the surface of a planet. Come to that – we risk our lives every time that we cross a busy street.'

'The Commodore,' said Clavering, 'wants our answer by 1300 hours today. There will be quite a deal of fitting out to be done if we accept the charter. So we'll vote on it now.'

'I still don't like it,' complained Rokovsky, but his hand was raised in assent with those of the others.

None of *Sally Ann*'s people was sorry to get away from Lorn. It is a dismal planet, perhaps the most dismal of all the Rim Worlds. It is always cold, and the wind is always blowing, and the air is always thick with dust and chemical fumes.

They were pleased, all of them, when the passengers, the personnel of the Combined Universities Expedition to Eblis, boarded, when the ramps were drawn up and in and the airlock doors closed. They were happy as they stood by at their various stations, as the last seconds ticked away to the authorised time of departure.

Clavering and his navigating officers sat in the control room, looking out at the dismal landscape – the low, brown hills, the heaps of slag, the untidy, unlovely huddle of shabby buildings that was the city of Port Forlorn. The sun shone blearily through the haze that was the work of Industrial Man as much as the work of Nature.

Clavering watched the sweep second hand of the chronometre, waited for the last reports to come in from all departments. Satisfied, 'Lift ship!' he ordered.

'Lift ship!' repeated Larwood.

Sally Ann trembled as the rockets fired, then the great bulk of her rose as though she, like her people, was glad to be getting away and clear from Lorn. Clavering could see the dirty concrete of the spaceport diminishing fast below them, cranes and gantries and the Rim Runners' tramp loading for Tharn looking like toys, the hulk of the unfortunate *Faraway Quest,* surrounded by the busy machines of the ship repair squads, looking like the body of some large insect being torn to pieces by voracious ants.

Clavering was sorry for *Faraway Quest* and for her Captain – but he was, at the same time, glad – his loyalties were to *Sally Ann*, and this charter, even though it was the direct result of another shipmaster's misfortune, could well mean her salvation.

She was clear of the atmosphere now, her rockets

silent, falling free in orbit about the dun, uninviting ball that was Lorn. To one side of her was the great glowing lens of the Galaxy, to the other the black emptiness of intergalactic space. Her gyroscopes whined as she turned slowly, as Larwood lined her up for the Eblis sun. Clavering was content to watch the efficient, unhurried actions of his Chief Officer; reckless he might be in some respects, but never in his ship handling or his navigation.

'Resume accelerations sir?' asked Larwood. 'One gravity for five minutes?'

'Resume acceleration,' replied Clavering.

Again the rockets roared, building up thrust and velocity. Larwood took observations and read instruments, assisted by the Second Officer, corrected *Sally Ann*'s trajectory with a brief burst from a steering jet. When he was satisfied he looked at Clavering, who nodded. Larwood cut the reaction drive, ordered the Mannschenn Drive to be started. The song of the spinning, precessing flywheels filled all the spaces of the ship; abruptly the Galactic lens took on the appearance of a huge, luminous Klein flask fashioned by a demented glass blower. Clavering felt, as always, the uncanny sensation of *déjà vu* as the temporal precession fields built up, the knowledge that past, present and future were one and indivisible. He wondered, as he always did on these occasions, if he possessed in some slight degree the talent of precognition. He tried, as he always did – and invariably without success – to foresee coming events.

'On trajectory, sir,' reported the Chief Officer.

'Thank you, Mr Larwood. Set deep space watches, observe standing orders.'

He unbuckled himself from his chair, pulled himself by the guide rail to the axial shaft. He wanted to see how Sally Ann was making out with the passengers and, more especially, with the almost untrained girls who had been engaged as stewardesses. He tried, for the last time, before his mind became accustomed to the time-twisting field of the Drive, to look into the future.

All that he could think of was what Grimes had said to him when he had been trying to arrange a charter: 'A man who'd come out to the Rim to earn his living would go to Hell for a pastime.'

It was a quiet trip.

The scientists kept very much to themselves and gave no trouble. There was no need for the ship's staff to organise entertainments, to keep the customers busy and, therefore, happy. The customers kept themselves busy, checking and rechecking their equipment, studying what little was known about the world to which they were bound, attending lectures given by the experts in various fields.

The only one of the party with whom Clavering had any real contact was Dr Fosdick, the leader of the expedition. He and the Master studied such maps and charts as existed – and incomplete and vague they were – and tried to work out some sort of plan of campaign.

'This is the plateau, Captain,' said Fosdick, his gnarled index finger stabbing at the paper. 'Observations from Space indicate that it is free from volcanic activity and not affected by earthquakes.'

'Can you see an earthquake from a thousand miles out?' asked Clavering dubiously. 'Remember that a ship on the ground is a fragile and top heavy thing, and a relatively slight tremor could well cause her total destruction.'

'The spring stays should take care of that,' Fosdick assured him. 'After all, Captain Calver, in *Lorn Lady*, rode out a hurricane on Melise – his ship was grounded for engine repairs – by using his stays.'

'I've heard all about that,' grumbled Clavering. 'I'm

beginning to wonder why the marvellous Captain Calver wasn't picked for this job. In any case – a hurricane is not an earthquake, and both are outside a spaceman's normal range of experience.'

'There are hurricanes as well as earthquakes on Eblis,' said Fosdick cheerfully, his teeth startlingly white in his gaunt, brown face as he grinned. 'You'll be used to both by the time we leave.'

'*If* we leave,' said Clavering gloomily.

'We'll leave all right. Now, this plateau. It's an ideal base for our operations, affording a good landing ground for both 'planes and helicopters. As far as we can see from the photographs from space there's a fairly gradual slope down to the south'ard – it's almost more of a bluff than a plateau, really – that out tractors will be able to negotiate. All that you have to do is to set the ship down somewhere in the middle of it.'

'Easier said than done,' remarked Clavering sarcastically.

He was far from happy about the project. He had been brought up in the big ships of the Trans-Galactic Clippers, in a service in which the biggest of all crimes is the hazarding of one's vessel. He had made landings only on planets with proper spaceports and adequate facilities. He had lived, until now, in an orderly Universe governed by wise rules and regulations. He was beginning to regret the winning of that huge lottery prize by the syndicate of which he was a member.

He said, 'I'll have to send down probe rockets first.'

'Of course, Captain. You're the spaceman – we're only passengers. The terms of your charter demand that you deliver us and our equipment on Eblis, that you maintain your ship as headquarters for the expedition. *How* you do it is up to you entirely.'

'I'll need the help of your people in evaluating the data obtained by the probes.'

'Of course.'

'And my requirements are a stable landing ground and no winds over fifty knots.'

'Now,' said Fosdick, 'you're asking too much.'

Yes, thought Clavering, he had been asking too much. He and Larwood sat strapped in their chairs in Control while Fosdick and his team correlated the data being sent up from the surface of the planet below them. He looked out through the ports at the huge, ruddily glowing sphere. Whoever had named it Eblis had not exaggerated. It seemed impossible that any life could survive on its fierily hostile crust for longer than five seconds at the outside, no matter what cunning aids existed. He heard Fosdick and his men and women exclaiming happily – happily! – over each fresh piece of evidence. 'Surface temperature 99.5 degrees Centigrade!' 'The wind force of seventy knots!' 'And what a wind! Straight hydrochloric acid gas!' 'The radiation count's surprisingly low . . .' This in tones of disappointment. 'Hullo! Free oxygen! What's that doing here?' 'No trace of it from *my* rocket.'

Larwood raised quizzical eyebrows. He murmured, 'We seem to have let ourselves in for something, sir.'

'You're telling me,' agreed the Captain. 'I thought that this was a good idea at the time we drew up the charter – now I'm not so sure.'

'Rokovsky's bellyaching as usual,' said Larwood. 'He's telling everybody that it'll be suicide to attempt a landing. Mary's quite keen, though. She has the idea that there might even be life of a sort on Eblis.'

'And all that Sally Ann's worried about is getting the hire money,' said Clavering.

Fosdick pulled himself over to them, handling himself in free fall with almost the ease of an experienced spaceman. He looked almost happy. He said, 'How soon can you take her down, Captain Clavering?'

'As soon as I get a detailed report from your bright boys

on what to expect,' replied Clavering. 'As soon as I get some data on wind velocities and on the nature of the terrain on the bluff, or the plateau, or whatever you've decided to call it. As soon as I can be assured that the ship won't be toppled over by an earth tremor as soon as she touches down.'

'That last assurance I can't give you,' said Fosdick.

'Then we don't land.'

'I appreciate your feelings,' said the scientist, 'but I must remind you that according to the terms of the charter party you receive no hire money whatsoever until the landing is made. If you've brought us here to have a look at Eblis from a safe distance then you, and you alone, are liable for the cost of our transportation for the round trip. Believe me, I hate having to hold a pistol at your head – but I have my job to do, just as you have yours.'

'Sally Ann should have had more sense when she arranged the charter,' said Larwood.

'We all read it,' said Clavering. 'Even Rokovsky was in agreement. And, after all, if we do lose the ship we don't lose financially.'

'There are such minor matters as our lives and our certificates to be considered,' said Larwood, grinning. 'Still, it's a gamble, and I'm one never to turn a gamble down.'

'I'm not a gambler,' replied Clavering shortly.

'Well, Captain?' demanded Fosdick impatiently.

'You heard what I said,' Clavering told him. 'I'm not a gambler. I've no intention on gambling that the earth tremors will hold off long enough for me to set *Sally Ann* down on her beautiful backside and for me to get the spring stays rigged.'

'So you refuse to land?'

'I never said that. I said that I wasn't gambling. I've devoted a great deal of thought to the landing problems; I never believed that your plateau was the ideal spot you said it was. I worked on the assumption that it wasn't – and, as far as I can gather, the probe rockets have borne me out.' He turned to his Mate. 'Mr Larwood – those stays are easily accessible, aren't they?'

'Of course, sir.'

'Then I'd like them shackled to the stem eyebolts right away. At the same time you can have numbers one and two boats ready for launching. You'll need four of those portable electric winches that Dr Fosdick has among his equipment – I'm assuming, Doctor, that you're willing to lend them to me ...'

'I don't see why I should.'

'Do you want to land on this literally blasted planet, or don't you?'

'I do, but I can't see . . .'

'As you keep on reminding me – I'm a spaceman. Now, Mr Larwood, these stays. I want them shackled on with the spring up. It's not the way they were supposed to be used, but it's the way that I'm using them.'

'Spring up, sir,' repeated Larwood.

'Good. Now, Dr Fosdick, I'm going to ask you for volunteers. As you know, we don't carry a large crew. We haven't the personnel for what I have in mind. I'll want at least six of your men, all in radiation armour.'

'You've thought of something,' grumbled the scientist, 'but what? And surely it would have been better if we had all discussed it in advance of our landing.'

'That,' said Clavering, 'was the one thing that I didn't want to do. Landing a big ship is essentially a one-man job. If he discusses the job first, other people will put forward their own schemes, some of them at least as good as his own. That way the seeds of doubt are sown and take root. That way, at a crucial moment there's just that second or so of hesitation, and the ship is lost. Understand one thing, please. I know what I'm going to do, and I think that it's the best way to do it.'

'I think that we should know what you're going to do, too,' said Fosdick. 'After all, if we volunteer we have a right to be told what risks we're running.'

'I take it that you're among the volunteers?' asked Clavering.

'Of course.'

'All right. As you are aware, it might well be that a sudden earth tremor, a sudden gust of wind, will overset the ship at the very moment of landing. She'll be safe enough once the spring stays are rigged – but quite a lot can happen while they're being rigged. This is my plan. I send two boats down in advance of the ship under my chief and second officers. Each boat will carry two of the portable winches, anchoring gear, and the volunteers. The volunteers will set up the winches and mark the landing site. We, in *Sally Ann*, will drop down as gently as possible, with the stays all ready to be fired to the ground by signal rockets. I considered landing with the stays trailing, but there's too much risk of their getting into the exhaust. As soon as the ends of the stays are on the ground they will be taken to the winches and heaved taut, and kept taut as the ship loses altitude. . . .'

'You're putting a lot of trust in the winches and the ground anchors,' said Fosdick.

'I have no option.'

'And you say that *I'm* a gambler!' exclaimed Larwood.

'A calculated risk is not a gamble,' replied Clavering stiffly. 'Now, Mr Larwood, you know what I want done, and why. I shall be obliged if you will begin making the necessary arrangements.'

'Ay, ay, sir,' replied Larwood smartly.

It should work, thought Clavering. *It must work. As far as I know, no landing of this nature has ever been attempted before – at least, not with a spaceship. I've seen something similar done on Chassor, where the natives use big, gas-filled airships for transport – but a spaceship is not an airship. Even so, I'm substituting thrust for buoyancy, so there's not all that much difference . . .*

The periscope showed him the terrain immediately below the ship. He could see the great daub of white pigment on the bare, red rock, the two boats well clear of it, the four winches, each standing in its own patch of white, the tiny, spacesuited figures of the two officers and the volunteers.

So far things were going well. He was finding it easy to keep Larwood's marker centred in the field of the periscope. Mary Larwood, with another three volunteers from among the scientists, was standing by in the airlock with the signal rockets, to which the thin, flexible but enormously strong stay wires had been shackled. To make a landing with an airlock door open was against all the rules of spacemanship – but in this case it had to be done.

Sally Ann was assisting in the control room; it was not the first time that she had done so. Short handed as the ship, her namesake, was, it had often been necessary for officers to perform duties outside their own departments. She was watching the radar, calling the altitude readings at short, measured intervals.

'Seven hundred . . . Six-fifty . . . Six hundred . . . Five-fifty . . .'

'Airlock!' barked Clavering. 'Fire one!'

'Fire one!' replied Mary Larwood's voice from the intercom speaker.

The missile came into the field of the periscope, trailing its plume of white exhaust smoke. It fell with deceptive slowness – the difference, thought Clavering, between objective and subjective time. It struck well clear of the winch for which it was aimed, burst in brief flame and flying fragments. Larwood's men pounced on it, took the end of the wire to the anchored winch.

'Fire two!' ordered Clavering.

'Fire two!'

The second rocket, to the Captain's dismay, was speeding straight for its target. He thought of increasing thrust to lift the ship, hoping thereby to twitch the line and throw the rocket out of its trajectory, knowing that with all the slack wire there was little hope that this could be done. His hand was about to descend on the firing keys when he saw the little rocket veer – it was, he learned later, an opportune gust of wind acting upon the vanes and the trailing line – and, it seemed to him, barely skim the winch. *A miss,* he thought relievedly, *is as good as a mile.*

Again Larwood and his men pounced, working with speed and efficiency.

'Landing party to *Sally Ann,*' came Larwood's voice, tinny and distorted, lacking depth. 'Chief Officer to *Sally Ann.* First and second wires on winches.'

'Up slack,' ordered Clavering. Then: 'Control to airlock. Fire three!'

'Fire three!'

There was a limited arc of fire from the outer door of the airlock; even so, Mary Larwood contrived to place the rocket well clear of the first two. Clavering watched Larwood's men – fewer of them now, two of them were standing by winch controls – carry the end of the wire to the third winch.

'Control to landing party,' he snapped. 'Up slack. Control to airlock. Fire four!'

After a short interval Larwood reported, 'All wires on winch barrels. Am taking up slack.'

The scene below the ship, in the periscope field, quivered, as though watched through disturbed water. Stupidly, Clavering looked at his gauges and meters, wondering what was wrong, why he felt no vibration, realised that he was watching a severe earth tremor. He saw the landing party stagger and fall, saw the men at the winches cling to their machines desperately. Through the ports he saw that, even so, an even tension was being maintained on all four stays. The tremor was worsening, though. The driver of the northernmost winch was thrown from the seat of his machine. He must have clutched at the control lever as he fell. The wire tightened. Looking up, Clavering watched the powerful spring at the ship's stem opening.

'Larwood!' he called urgently.

Larwood had scrambled to his feet, was running unsteadily towards the runaway machine. The Second Officer, who had risen to a sitting position, was waving to the other drivers, making circling motions with his arms, obviously signalling to them to open up their own controls to maximum speed.

It was the southern winch that took the strain first – and as the weight came on it a dark fissure opened in the rock directly under it, directly in way of the screw pile anchor. The machine lurched over the ground, spilling its operator, climbing up its own wire.

Sally Ann tilted dangerously, in the direction of the overtaut stay to the northward.

When in doubt,

Get Out!

The words of the old spaceman's rhyme flashed through Clavering's mind. But he couldn't get out. He was secured to the surface of the planet by three strong wires, by three screw piles. If he applied maximum thrust the wire *might* break or the piles pull out, at the risk of considerable damage to the ship and, even worse, severe casualties to the landing party.

He cut the drive.

Sally Ann fell sickeningly. The red rocks rushed up to meet her, to crush her.

Clavering's hands fell heavily on the firing keys. The ship shuddered under maximum thrust, shuddered and checked her descent, started to lift. Swiftly, Clavering reduced the power of his thundering jets, held the ship balanced there, thrust cancelling but not overcoming gravity. He realised that the wire of the runaway winch had sagged into the incadescent exhaust and had been parted, saw that the other three were once again under full control. He knew that there were now only three stays, and those not placed to the best advantage.

'Rokovsky,' he said into the intercom. 'I want you to get another wire along into the airlock, and I want it shackled on to the stem as soon as we touch. Larwood!'

'Sir?' answered the Chief Officer.

'You heard what I told Rokovsky. Can that winch and the screw pile be used again?'

'That winch is tough,' replied Larwood, 'and the thread of the pile's undamaged.'

'Good. Get them set up again as near as possible to the old place. Is the tremor over?'

'Yes.'

'Maintain the tension on the other stays. I'm coming in.'

He dropped the ship without undue haste, yet without undue caution, careful, however, to defer landing until the winch was once again anchored. At the first quiver that told of contact with the surface he cut the drive. He sat back in his chair, conscious at last of the perspiration that had soaked his garments, grateful when Sally Ann got up from her own seat to stand beside him, her hand on his shoulder. He watched the spacesuited figures clambering up the hull outside the control room ports, heard faintly the clang of their armoured feet and hands in the recessed rungs. He saw the wire snaking up after them, saw Larwood and his people running with the free end of it to the winch. He felt the ship tremble as, after what seemed an unconscionably long delay, the weight came on it.

Only then could he begin to relax, could he stare out of

the ports at the desolate landscape, at the barren rocks, at the distant, heavily smoking, flaring volcanoes, at the ruddy sky with its glowing, ominous clouds scudding before the gale.

'Even so,' said Sally Ann, 'it's not as bad as Lorn.'

Clavering, who had come to hate that planet during his vessel's long stay on its surface, agreed.

They were not long on the plateau.

Fosdick had lost no time in sending out his exploring parties, both by land and by air. It had been the party that he was leading that had found the valley, an oasis in the burning aridity of the north polar regions. There was life in the valley – as, in fact, there was in many other regions of Eblis – both plant and animal. The surrounding hills shielded the valley from the noxious gales and the atmosphere was breathable by humans. There was a level plain, beside a river of barely lukewarm water, on which a ship could land. The valley was a paradise compared with most of the planet – and it was like a medieval artist's conception of Hell.

Clavering, not reluctantly, had lifted the ship from the plateau, had taken her to the valley. It had been necessary to repeat the manoeuvre with the stay wires and winches – the new landing place and base was not free from earth tremors – but this time the operation had been carried out without mishap.

The time set for the expedition's return to Lorn approached.

Clavering, taking one last walk through the valley with Sally Ann, decided that he would be sorry to leave the place. It was pleasant to walk abroad without a spacesuit, lightly attired in shorts and shirt uniform, to feel the warm air on bare skin, to breathe that same air and to appreciate the not unpleasant tang given it by the diluted fumes from the distant volcanoes. There were no volcanoes in the valley itself – only two huge pillars of flaming, roaring natural gas and a half dozen spectacular geysers.

By the river they walked, the steam from the warm water billowing about them, obscuring and still further distorting the outline of the rocks tortured into towering, grotesque shapes by some long ago volcanic acticity. Past trees and shrubs they walked, past the plants with their gnarled, convoluted trunks and stems, with the broad, jagged edged leaves that were black rather than green, over grass of the same sombre hue. But there was colour in the crimson river and the crimson sky, in the clumps of monstrous fungi, misshapen monstrosities in orange and lemon yellow. Overhead, black, ragged silhouettes against the glowing sky, flapped the flying things, more bird than reptile, croaking dismally. A tribe of 'devils' – horned, scaly beings built on the same lines as the Terran kangaroo – hopped to meet them, hold out their claws for the candies that the explorers had learned to carry in their pockets.

'This place is frightening,' said Sally Ann, 'but it's not frightening in the real sense of the word, not any longer. It's like. . . . It's like the scary rides and so on in a Fun Palace. You pay good money to be scared – but, all the time, at the back of your mind you aren't scared. You know it's all make-believe. It's the same here. There's scenery like an old time artist's idea of Hell – the river could be a river of blood and these rocks could be the damned themselves, writhing in perpetual torment. Then we have the devils. . . .' She paused to give some more candy to the most persistent of them. 'We have the devils, the most evil looking beasts that I've seen on any world I've visited – and all that they're good for is scrounging chocolate. . . .

'You know,' she went on, 'people pay to see far less convincing shows than this – and we're getting paid for seeing it. Oh well, we'd better make the most of it. We have to take our load of scientists back to Lorn, and then we'll be back in the real Hell – the one in which we have to make enough money, somehow, to keep the ship running. When this character expires there'll be nothing for us on the Rim. . . .'

'So everybody keeps on telling me,' said Clavering. 'And Grimes told me something else, too. I've just remembered it.'

'What was it?' she asked.

'Just one of the Rim World proverbs,' he said.

She was a large hunk of ship was *Sally Ann*, too large and too imposing for the name she bore. She stood proudly in her berth at Port Forlorn, dwarfing cranes and gantries and administration buildings, towering high above *Rimgirl* and *Rimbird*, both typical units of the Rim Runners' fleet.

Commodore Grimes, Astronautical Superintendent for Rim Runners, looked out from the window of his office towards the big ship, screwing his eyes against the steely glare of the westering sun. There was a certain admiration showing on his hard, pitted face as he said, 'So you've done it, Captain. You're making that big white elephant of yours pay for her feed bills. . . .'

'And there's a little left over for us,' said Clavering, watching the embarking passengers moving up the ramp in a wonderfully steady stream.

'You'll have had expenses,' said Grimes. 'Setting up a permanent holiday camp on Eblis, for a start. And your advertising . . .'

'Your people did most of that for us,' said Clavering. 'Those excellent films made by the expedition have been showing to packed houses on all the Rim Worlds. As for the rest of it – the Universities are sharing the expense and, of course, the profits, which will help to finance their further explorations of Eblis.'

'How did you think of it?' asked Grimes.

'It was something my wife said our last night in the valley. You've seen the films of it – it's a weird place, rather terrifying, yet with no real danger whatsoever. Even if there's an earthquake, the grass is soft, and the inflatable houses we've shipped out are earthquake proof anyhow. She said it was like those scary sideshows in Fun Palaces – haunted houses and the like – that people pay good money to enter. They like to be frightened, as long as they know that it's make-believe fright. Too, it's a change from Lorn and Faraway, Ultimo and Thule . . . Yes, and it was something that you said, too, that put me on to it.'

'And what was that, Captain Clavering?'

'"A man who comes out to the Rim to make his living,"' quoted Clavering, '"would go to hell for a pastime."'

Wet Paint

In all probability you've never heard of Kinsolving – most people, and that includes the majority of spacemen, have not. It's one of the Rim Worlds, which means that it's well off the beaten track even for the Commission's Epsilon-class tramps. It's an Earth-type planet, but not sufficiently similar to Earth to make it attractive to colonists. The gravity is a little too heavy and the air is a little too thin and a little too rich in carbon dioxide. Its sun is hot enough, but not very bright, and its light is so blue as to convey the impression of chilliness. Then, of course, there is that aching emptiness of the night sky for six months of the year without even a moon to take the curse off it.

Kinsolving, then, is just a name in the Survey Commission's files – just a name and a few lines of relevant data. Discovered and charted by Commodore Pearson of the Survey Ship *Magellan*, named after his second-in-command. Survey team left on planet, taken off after the usual two years of exploration and research. Colony established, complete with machinery and necessary flora and fauna. After ten years colony removed, at its own request, and transferred to Clarency, q.v.

'What do you know about Kinsolving?' Warburton asked me.

Warburton is my immediate superior and is the Director of the Survey Commission's little publicised Department of Investigation. Boiled down to essentials his job is to read reports – reports written by captains of

Survey ships, by masters of the Interstellar Transport Commission's vessels and, now and again, by the masters of ships owned by those few alien races that meet us on equal terms on a technological level. Sometimes he finds something of interest in these reports – and when he does he sends an investigatory team which, in its turn, makes out its own report. What happens next is up to the high brass.

'What do you know about Kinsolving?' he asked again.

'Rear Admiral, Retired,' I said. 'Useful but undistinguished career. That's all.'

'Not the man,' snapped Warburton. 'The planet. He had a world named after him. Look it up, Tarrant.'

I looked it up. I dialled the Central Library, said what I wanted, and in a matter of seconds Warburton and I were watching the pitifully few paragraphs of printed matter glowing on the screen.

'A typical Rim World,' I said. 'Rather worse than most, perhaps.'

'I have a report here,' said Warburton, 'from one Captain Spence, Master of *Epsilon Eridani*. She was on charter for a while to Thule Lines. She was en route from Elsinore to Ultimo when she had trouble with her Drive – and, as you know, the Mannschenn Drive controls can be recalibrated only on a planetary surface. The nearest planet was Kinsolving and Spence landed there, at the old spaceport. Anyhow, you can read.' He handed me the sheaf of papers. 'See what you make of it.'

I sat down and read the report. Reports made by shipmasters, I have found, fall invariably into either one or the other of two categories. They are either tersely official or too, too literary. It was soon obvious to me that Captain Spence fancied himself as a latter-day Conrad.

'The derelict spaceport buildings looked, in that livid light, like tombstones in a deserted graveyard,' he wrote.

'A little to the south lay the town, obviously dead. It was hard to believe that it had ever been inhabited. The only visible movement was that of the smoke and steam drifting in ragged streamers up past our Control Room ports – the apron, as we had noticed from the air prior to our landing, was overgrown with some tough, indigenous creeping plant, the tendrils of which had been incinerated by the backblast of our Interplanetary Drive.

'I looked at Makins, my Chief Officer. Something of my feelings, must have shown in my expression. He looked at me and said, "Fine place for a funeral, Captain."'

So it went on. I skipped a few pages of rich, beautiful atmospheric writing. Then:

'Laurencon, the Interstellar Drive Engineer, told me that the work of recalibration would take at least six days, local time. On hearing this Mr Makins asked my permission to break out the helicopter and, accompanied by a party of junior officers and cadets, to carry out an exploration of his own. He assured me that no dangerous animals existed on Kinsolving, and a copy of Commodore Pearson's report, which had been put aboard, together with other useful literature by the management of Thule Lines, bore him out. He said that it was probable that some of the pigs and rabbits brought by the colonists had survived and pointed out that meat in our tissue culture vats had become rather flavourless. He said that he wished to find some of the caves reported by the original survey team and to take photographs of the paintings on their walls. He even thought that his own unskilled investigations might do something towards solving the mystery of the disappearance of the long-ago humanoids who had produced those paintings. I was reluctant at first to give my permission, then remembered that it is the duty of every shipmaster to further the work of interstellar survey when by so doing he does not endanger either his own ship or her personnel. I told him to go ahead with his preparations.

'Mr Makins is an efficient officer, and by early afternoon of that same day he had everything ready. The helicopter was assembled and standing on the apron, looking like some huge, ungainly insect. Its storage space was packed with provisions and ammunition for the light sporting rifles that all of us carried; on the Rim Worlds there is little in the way of amusement and hunting is one way of spending one's shore leave. He had chosen to accompany him Wallis, the Third Officer, and Penrod and Gilbey, two of the cadets.

'He told me that he planned to take the helicopter to the foothills of the McIvor Range, in the valleys of which the caves with the paintings had been found. He said that he would keep in touch with the ship by means of the helicopter's radio telephone and that he had already drawn up a schedule of times with Mr Cade, the Radio Officer. I made sure that he and his party had everything that they were likely to need – there were, however, a very few suggestions that I could make – then stood back and watched as the little flowers of flame blossomed at the tips of the rotor blades, as the ungainly contraption lifted and in its graceless way flew to the westward, to the dull blue serrated line of the Range in silhouette against the dull blue sky, the bright metal of it gleaming drearily in the light of that dreary blue sun.'

'And they called it the birth of the blues,' I muttered.

'What was that?' demanded Warburton. He grinned. 'Yes, Captain Spence's prose is rather overpowering at times. But read on.'

I read on.

'That night Makins called the ship at the appointed time. He had little to report. He had shot a pig, and he and his party were supping off roast pork. He had found the entrances to several promising looking caves but, so far, had deferred investigation. I rather gained the impression that the real purpose of his expedition had been to get away from the deadly monotony of ship's food.

'He called again the following morning. He said that he was about to commence his exploration of the caves. I told him to make sure that he used the balls of twine that he had taken to mark his inward track; he replied rather curtly that as he had thought of those balls of twine he was not likely to forget their purpose. At noon young Penrod called the ship, telling me that the others were still in the caves and that he had been left at the camp to cook the mid-day meal. They were having rabbit, he said, and sweet corn, a goodly supply of which was growing wild near where the helicopter had landed.

'The next call was scheduled for late afternoon. I was in the Radio Room waiting for it to come through, but I was expecting little more, by this time, than a detailed account of the day's meals. Makins's voice, however, was excited.

'"Captain," he said "we've found the paintings!"

'"Good," I replied. "Did you get photographs?" He ignored my question.

'"Captain!' he almost shouted, "the paint is *wet*!"

'"Mr Makins," I said, "a Survey Team spent all of two years on this planet. Had there been intelligent life here they must surely have found it. Perhaps your wet paint is due to seepage of moisture from the cave roof."

'He replied with a rude monosyllable. Then, "Sir," he said stiffly. "I'm mate of a ship. I know something about paint and painting. It's part of my job. If I say that the paint is wet, it *is* wet. I am returning to the spaceport at once, and I suggest that you come with me in the helicopter to see for yourself."

'I was waiting outside when the helicopter returned. The sun was down, but we saw its navigation lights and the red exhaust flames when it was still a few miles distant; they stood out sharply and brightly against the black, almost starless sky. All of us, except the engineers who were working on the recalibration of the Drive controls, were waiting outside. News spreads very fast through a ship.

'The helicopter landed. We stood back until the vanes had almost stopped whirring, then almost ran to the door of the cabin. Makins was the first out. He stood there mutely and showed me his hands. The palms were smeared with black and ochre. There was a strong smell of vegetable oil and other, unidentifiable smells that must have come from the pigments used. I touched Makins's right palm with the index finger of my own right hand. The tip of my finger was stained black.

'"Mr Makins," I asked, "is this a hoax?"

'"I am not a first-trip cadet," he replied. "I have learned that a sense of humour does little to aid one's promotion."

'He was rather annoyed when I told him that Mr Wallis would pilot me back to the cave and that he would have to remain with the ship. Regulations make it quite clear that on planets with no proper port facilities – and surely Kinsolving comes into that category! – either the Mate or the Master must be aboard at all times. He told me that he had left a good fire burning in the valley and that Mr Wallis would have no trouble in finding the landing place. So it proved to be.

'It was cold in the valley – in spite of the fire – and dark. The little river running down it chuckled and gurgled over the stones of its bed, sounding uncomfortably like voices. Something was rustling in the bushes. A pig, perhaps, or one of the large, harmless herbivorous mammals native to the planet, or one of the predatory lizards. According to the Survey Team and according to the colonists these lizards never attacked Man, but there has to be a first time for everything.

'At its upper end the valley was more of a canyon, and

that is where the caves were. Wallis took a torch from the cabin of the helicopter and guided me over the rough ground. The two cadets tailed along behind.

'We found the mouth of the cave without any difficulty. The end of the ball of twine shone white in the light of our torches; it was made fast to a bush. The cave itself was all of seven feet from floor to ceiling and must once have had a stream flowing through it; there was a fair thickness of fine white sand on its floor. For about fifty feet we walked, descending gradually. Then, after a sharp turn, we came into the first chamber. On the walls were the paintings. I have seen photographs of similar work by primitive artists on Earth and other humanoid-inhabited worlds. They all run very much to pattern. They all, or almost all, depict hunting scenes. There are the hunters with their spears or bows, sometimes their dogs. There is the mammoth of the buffalo, or its other-worldly equivalent, resembling an animated pin-cushion. There is the peculiar blend of crudity and sophistication that is inevitable when the artist has yet to learn his craft.

'It was all very impressive. I walked to the nearer of the paintings, put out an experimental finger.

'"Mr Wallis," I said, "it is obvious, even to me, that these paintings were made at least thousands of years ago."

'"These, sir," he said, "are not *the* paintings."

'He led us along what seemed at least another two miles of tunnel. We came at last into another chamber, larger than the first. Its walls, too, were covered with paintings. The hunting theme was again predominant.

'And the paint was wet.'

I looked up from the report.

'That initial Survey Team must have made a very poor job,' I said.

'Initial Survey Teams just don't make very poor jobs,'

said Warburton, 'ever. If the Initial Survey Team said that there was no intelligent life on the planet – then there *was* no intelligent life on the planet. When you finish reading Captain Spence's report you will find that the wet paint was the only evidence of intelligent life found by the crew of *Epsilon Eridani*. She couldn't stay after the recalibration of her Drive controls was completed – Captain Spence was bound by the terms of the second charter – but her people used every remaining second of the period of their stay on Kinsolving to try to find the answer to the riddle. Spence took scrapings of paint both from the old and the new paintings. They have been analysed. The old paint is *old* – at least fifty thousand years. The new paint was mixed only a few months ago. The oil was not, as he assumed, of vegetable origin, but animal. The pigments were powdered charcoal and an ochreous earth.'

'So,' I asked, 'what?'

'So we are sending our team of investigators,' he told me. 'This is all part and parcel of the ... the general queerness that you find out at the Rim. The Rim governments aren't interested – they never are unless there's money involved. So it's our baby.'

'Who are you sending?' I asked.

'The Rhine Institute will supply an Esper if I ask them nicely. Then there's Rizzio, our own tame gunman. An ethnologist might not come amiss. There seems to be scope for a speleologist. Then, of course, we must have the usual man in the street who has knocked around a bit and who is not entirely devoid of imagination as coordinator. That's where you come in.'

'That's what I feared,' I said.

'You don't like the Rim, do you?' he asked.

'Who does? There's that feeling that all the time that you're on the very edge of *something* – or *nothing*. I'm never sure which of the two is worse.'

'You'd better start getting packed and saying your goodbyes,' he said. 'If you catch *Alpha Draconis* next week you'll get out to Thule in under three months. If you miss her it means a roundabout route, mainly in Delta- and Epsilon-class tramps and, possibly, an occasional Shaara ship. As it is, the *Alfie Dragon* can't take you all the way. Her terminal planet's Mergenwiler.'

So I made a start by handing things over to my immediate inferior, a youth called Jones. I wondered how the office would manage without me. There were only four of us in the Department in those days – Warburton, Rizzio, Jones and myself.

The next day Warburton was in a bad temper. He had succeeded in persuading the Rhine Institute to lend us an Esper free of charge – after all, the Institute is usually only too grateful to be allowed to poke its collective nose into anything smacking of paranormal phenomena. The grounded Commodore who was his superior had refused, however, to sanction the expense of hiring any of the experts that he had considered necessary for the job. The team, then, was to consist of Rizzio, the Esper and myself.

Rizzio, who had been called into his office for instructions, wasn't worried about it. He believed – and not without cause – that there was no possible jam in the Universe out of which he could not shoot his way. His favourite weapons were a pair of beautifully balanced, beautifully inlaid point five automatics, although in his hands a little Minetti needle gun was equally deadly. But Rizzio liked the feel of the heavier weapons, liked the kick of them, the roar of them. For the various radiation pistols he had nothing but contempt. 'These,' he would say, pulling his big automatics with a lightning movement, 'will always knock a man down no matter what sort of armour he's wearing or what sort of screen he's using. Those other toys will only give him a mild case of sunburn.'

That then, was Rizzio, a little man with all of the little man's aggressiveness, a little man elevated to giant's stature by virtue of the weapons that he handled with such assured mastery. I liked him, but I was a little afraid of him. I was always conscious of the viciousness that I had seen, more than once, transform the dark, normally pleasantly smiling face into a snarling, feral mask.

We sat there – Warburton, Rizzio, Jones and myself – drinking coffee from the automatic dispenser and smoking. We advanced various theories to account for the still-wet cave painting – Jones, I remember, insisted on calling Central Library for information about some hoax in the Twentieth Century involving some allegedly prehistoric but actually non-existent being called Piltdown Man. The cave paintings, he said, could well be a similar hoax.

There was a tap at the door.

'Come in!' called Warburton.

The girl who entered looked out of place in our dingy office. She was a little taller than the average and slim with the deceptive slenderness of the professional model. Her sleek hair was burnished copper and her eyes were green rather than grey. Her face was thin and finely modelled, with a wide, generous mouth. She was dressed with the extreme simplicity that looks far more expensive than deliberate, would-be impressive sumptuousness.

'Commander Warburton?' she asked.

Warburton got to his feet, as we all did.

'Yes. I am Warburton. What can I do for you, Miss . . .?'

'Wells, Sarah Wells. The Rhine Institute sent me.'

So this, I thought, is the Esper. My experience of women with psionic gifts has been that they run to fat, with puddingy faces and poor complexions. This Sarah Wells must be the exception that proved the rule.

'Coffee, Miss Wells?' Jones was falling over himself like a puppy eager to please. 'Cigarette?'

'Thank you.'

She took a cigarette from Jones' case with the slender fingers of her right hand, put it to her lips. She ignored Jones' lighter. The end of the little cylinder glowed suddenly into incandescence.

Warburton refused to be impressed.

'What other qualifications have you?' he asked. 'No doubt you've heard what the job is. It calls for something else than the ability to light a fire without matches.

'They class me as a GP,' replied the girl, 'General Purpose. I could get a job as a Psionic Communications Officer, I suppose. I have limited precognition. Telekinesis to a certain extent, although without sufficent control to make me an adept. Telemetering . . .'

'You'll do,' said Warburton, 'You'll do. We don't know what we're looking for, so an all-rounder like yourself is better than a specialist.'

'You flatter me,' she said, 'but I hope to be of service.'

We saw little of each other in the short time that remained to us before the departure of *Alpha Draconis*. Each of us had his own private affairs to put in order, his own farewells to make. Each day we would report to Warburton by videophone to see if there were any fresh developments, but there were none. Rizzio, I know, spent most of his spare time on the pistol range trying to improve upon the near perfection that was already his.

And then, one chilly morning, I was at the airport to catch the rocket mail for Port Woomera. I met Rizzio in the waiting room. He was as cocky as ever and full of the praises of the new hundred shot Minetti that he had bought. We saw the girl come in, escorted by a half-dozen scholarly looking men. Warburton came in, his bald head gleaming in the lamplight. He saw us, hurried across to us. He took us to where the girl was standing with the people from the Institute. There were hasty introductions, and then the impersonal voice of the announcer was telling all passengers to board Flight 306 for Port Woomera and we were walking out to the stratosphere rocket, leaving Warburton and Sarah Well's colleagues at the door of the waiting room. In silence we climbed the ramp into the long fuselage, in silence we allowed the stewardess to lead us to our seats. None of us was feeling in a conversational mood. I was placed next to the girl, Rizzio sat across the aisle. We survived, as one usually does, the initial, brutal acceleration. We looked out of the ports at the wide expanse of cloud and at the almost black sky above it. We revived slightly when coffee was served, and talked in a desultory manner of unimportant things. I learned that Sarah had never left Earth, had never, even, been as far afield as the Moon. She was a little scared of this adventure that would take us out to the very edge of the Galaxy.

Rizzio broke into the conversation.

'There is nothing to worry about,' he said. 'I have my guns with me, and they shoot as well at the Rim as on Earth.'

'But you are worried,' she said, with disconcerting directness. 'Both of you. You're scared of the Rim. From your minds I get the impression of the edge of darkness, and the fear that you will fall over that edge.'

'Nobody's done it yet,' I said.

'There has to be a first time,' said Rizzio cheerfully.

Then we were sliding down into denser atmosphere and Woomera was below us – the yellow desert, the white buildings and the silver starships. In seconds the silver ships became more than toys, became great, sky-piercing steeples towering high above our plane as she touched down. From a retractable gaff high on one of the metallic towers fluttered a square of blue and white bunting – the Blue Peter. In gleaming gold and green and crimson on her sleek side sprawled the winged dragon. The cargo ports, I noticed, were closed, and only a trickle of stores and baggage was running up into the vast hull along the one conveyor belt still in operation.

This, then, was *Alpha Draconis.* This was the ship that would take us two-thirds of the way to Thule.

We disembarked at Port Caterick on Mergenwiler, waiting there a week for *Delta Gemini.* Rizzio went out into the forest every day – Mergenwiler is a jungly world – with his precious guns, getting in what he considered valuable practice on the local fauna, especially the *kreeks,* six-legged lizard things well known for their speed and agility. As they are also well known for their depredations on the livestock imported by the colonists Rizzio became very popular. Sarah spent most of her time in the Psionic Radio office at the spaceport. Some days I went out with Rizzio, other days I accompanied Sarah. Being neither a gunsel nor a telepath I wasn't sorry when the *Dratted Twins,* as she was affectionately called, dropped down from the cloudy sky to the apron.

The *Dratted Twins* took us to Waverley, where all of us enjoyed watching the pomp and ceremony of that rather absurd little autonomous, Jacobean kingdom. From Waverley we travelled in *Flora Macdonald* to Elsinore, one of the planets in the so-called Shakespearean Sector, and from Elsinore *Lost Horizon* carried us to Thule.

We were out on the Rim now, and all of us knew it. It was the wrong time of the year on Thule, the time of the year when the night sky was empty of all the dim and incredibly distant nebulosities that were island universes. It was the time of the year when hardly anybody went out at night, and when those who did so kept their eyes on the ground and never looked up to the forlorn heavens. It was the time of the year when Man's primordial fear of the dark reasserted itself, when the dread of the black nothingness outside was almost palpable.

It hit Rizzio, and it hit me, but it hit Sarah hardest of all. 'It's the emptiness pressing in,' she said. 'Can emptiness press, Jim? Doesn't it make nonsense of all that you've ever learned of physics? But this emptiness presses – or it may be that our expanding galaxy is pressing against *it* ... It's the fear. Everybody is telepathic after a fashion, you know, and the fear builds up. These Rim Worlds are no more than vast psionic amplifiers, far more powerful than those pitiful dogs' brains we use in the ships and the shore stations.'

I pulled her to me and held her tightly. We were by ourselves in my room at the Rimrock Hotel – Rizzio had found a pistol range and working off his unease in a thunderous practice session. I held her tightly, and it was the first time in all the long voyage out from Earth that I had touched her. I felt comfort in her nearness. I like to think that she felt comfort in mine.

'This helps a little,' she said, 'but only a little. The fear is still there, the fear and the loneliness.'

'Are you sure that you want to go through with this?' I asked. 'Luigi and I can carry on – after all, we're officers of the Survey Service and under orders. You're not. The *Sundowner* blasts off tomorrow for Nova Caledon, and she'll take you well on your way back to Earth.'

She thrust her way out of my arms.

'What do you take me for?' she demanded. 'You and Luigi may be officers of the Survey Service – but I'm a graduate of the Rhine Institute – and never once has any of us run from the Unknown.'

I said, 'I'm glad you're staying. But I wish you weren't.'

'Why are you glad? So that this investigation of yours can proceed with my help?'

'No. Personal reasons. And the same applies to my

wishing that you'd get out of here and back to somewhere safe.'

'I'd be lying,' she said, 'if I told you that this was all a big surprise. You aren't a very good transmitter, but you're good enough at close range. It's rather a pity, darling, that you can't receive what I'm thinking ...'

'You can tell me,' I said, taking her in my arms again.

She was telling me when Rizzio came back, and the continuation of all she wanted to say had to be deferred to a later date.

Getting from Thule to Kinsolving wasn't easy. The Rim Worlds are dependent upon shipping, but there is very little traffic along the Rim itself. The Governor of Thule promised us every assistance – but there was very little assistance that he could give. Frankly, I wasn't much worried about it. I was with Sarah, and we knew how we felt about each other, and I was willing to wait ten years, if needs be, for transport. Unluckily Sarah didn't share my sentiments – on the transport question, that is. She was very much a Woman With A Mission and would never be really happy until the mission was accomplished. It was worse for her, of course, than it was for me. She was the telepath. I felt only the vague unease but she was conscious all the time of that all-pervading fear of the dark. That fear of hers was dangerous, too, especially at night when she half awoke and subconsiously used her pyrotic powers to dispel the darkness. I got into the habit of making sure that there was absolutely nothing of an inflammable nature in her room before I left her each night.

Rizzio was getting impatient, too.

'I've lugged my guns more than halfway across the Galaxy,' he would growl. 'I want to use 'em on something better than paper targets.'

Then, after we had been on Thule for over three weeks,

the *Lady Faraway* dropped in. She had been an Epsilon-class tramp owned by the Commission. She was still a tramp, but now wore the house-flag of Rim Runners, Incorporated, a one-ship company. Her Master was a retired Survey Service commander and proved sympathetic and helpful. Between us we worked out a plan of campaign. I would blast off in a second-hand lifeboat at the same time as *Lady Faraway*, making a rendezvous with her in orbit around Thule. We would then secure the boat to the ship, and *Lady Faraway* would break off her journey from Thule to Ultimo long enough to cast us off within easy rocket range of Kinsolving. On her return to Thule, two weeks later, she would pick us up. Sarah was confident of her ability to keep in touch with the tramp's Psionic Radio Officer.

That was the scheme, and it worked. Luigi and Sarah rode with me in the boat – such craft are just a little large to operate single-handed, especially when there is any spatial manoeuvring to be done. We made our rendezvous with *Lady Faraway* without any trouble. We pulled ourselves across the small gap between the two craft and, in a matter of minutes, were in the tramp's control room staring out at the shimmering glory of the Galactic lens. After that dismal night sky on Thule we couldn't see enough of it.

The voyage to Kinsolving passed pleasantly enough. Most of the time we were content to sip our drinks and let the skipper tell us stories about the Rim, stories that bore out what Warburton had said about the general oddness that exists in that part of the Galaxy. The most fantastic thing, however, was the way in which the Rim Dwellers seemed to take them for granted. The occasional phantom ship in their skies was no more to them than a rainbow in our skies is to us. The queer wreckage that fell on Faraway was melted down and broken up long before anybody thought of making a proper investigation. The ship from nowehere that appeared off Dunsinane and that was commandeered and manned by the people of that planet, only to vanish into the nothingness from which it had come, was practically laughed off as just one of those things.

'You get this way out on the Rim,' said the Captain, sensing our bewilderment. 'If you didn't, you'd be round the bend in next to no time. If I'd been Captain Spence I shouldn't have considered a spot of wet paint anything worth writing home about.'

'But it was *odd*,' I said.

'Everything out here is odd. I have my own private theory, and that is that Heisenberg's Uncertainty Principle is the only law of nature that's valid in these parts.'

'And how does it apply to wet paint?' I asked.

'Like this, Lieutenant. Twenty thousand years ago a caveman painted two pictures. One died, the other one didn't.'

'It doesn't satisfy me,' I said.

'Or me,' said Sarah.

'When I take aim,' said Luigi, 'it'd take more than the Uncertainty Principle to make the bullet go elsewhere than where it was supposed to.'

'There are such things as misfires,' said the Captain.

I've often wondered if he was really serious about his pet theory. It didn't seem to apply to his own navigation. *Lady Faraway* flickered back into the normal continuum no more than a thousand miles out from Kinsolving and, after we had bidden our hosts farewell, we transferred from the ship to the boat.

I had charts of the planet and was able to find the spaceport, which was in the daylit hemisphere, without trouble. When we hit the outer fringes of the atmosphere Sarah received a message from the ship to say that she would stand by until we had actually landed. When the boat touched down on the patch of lighter, newer green that marked the place where Captain Spence's *Epsilon Eridani* had incinerated the growth covering the apron, Sarah told *Lady Faraway* that we were safely down.

'Good luck,' they told us. 'Good hunting.'

We opened the door of the little airlock and climbed down to the ground. It was late afternoon of a fine day – fine, but oppressive. It may have been the heavy gravity, it may have been the excess of carbon dioxide in the atmosphere. It may have been something else. In any case, a derelict spaceport with a ghost town in the middle distance is not conducive to cheerfulness.

We had with us a helicopter – a flimsy, collapsible affair but capable of carrying three people, with their supplies, for not too great a distance. The remainder of the day we spent assembling the brute. I am not, I admit, an engineer. As far as Rizzio was concerned the only machinery for which he had any aptitude was of the lethal variety. I hate to have to admit it, but Sarah did most of the work. Tools behaved themselves in her hands. Nuts seemed almost to tighten themselves. Perhaps they did. Her telekinetic talent was of value.

When it was dark we made a meal from our self-heating cans of food. We were all tired. We wasted no time in getting to bed. Sarah and I slept in the boat, Luigi arranged his sleeping bag below the landing gear. I remember that he grinned whitely and patted the butts of his holstered automatics and said that they were the best bed companions on a world like Kinsolving. Sarah was rather shocked and annoyed when I laughed; I thought for a while that she was going to make me keep Rizzio company.

Sarah slept badly – which meant that I did too.

She said, 'I wish that I could explain it to you – but it's like trying to explain visual images to a blind man. How can I put it? It's like what I felt on Thule, the fear of the dark, but more intense. Much more intense. Could it be, do you think, that somehow the psychic emanations of all the Rim Worlds are focused here on Kinsolving?'

'You, my darling, are the expert,' I said.

She told me that I was no help at all. Then, after a little while, she woke me up again.

'There was a colony here,' she said. 'They were taken off at their own request. Why?'

'As far as I can gather, they just didn't like it here,' I said.

'They felt the same as I am feeling,' she said, 'and it was strong enough, even with non-telepaths, to make them clamour for evacuation.'

'Could be,' I said.

'You're the coordinator,' she told me.

'Even coordinators must sleep,' I told her.

And so it went on. When the morning came the pair of us were like pieces of chewed string. Rizzio was bright and breezy and repeated his remark about bed companions. Neither of us really thought it was funny.

We loaded the flimsy helicopter and climbed into the little cabin. I was rather surprised that the thing lifted, but it did so, albeit with a marked reluctance. We flew low – we had no option – following the route marked on Captain Spence's chart. We saw little of interest, the scenery in general was too Earthlike. In any case, I was spending all my time praying that the collapsible aircraft wouldn't collapse in midair.

We found the valley – it was the only one with a deep canyon at its upper end. We landed by the river. We unloaded from the helicopter what we would need – the powerful torches, the camera, the balls of twine, a Minetti automatic apiece for Sarah and myself. Luigi, of course, was wearing his usual assortment of personal artillery. He would have looked naked without it. Both Sarah and I felt, as we thrust the little pistols into the holsters at our belts, that we were wearing fancy dress.

We found the cave.

The end of the ball of twine paid out by the Mate of *Epsilon Eridani* was still there. We squabbled a little as to which of us should take the lead. Finally, I was able to convince the others that as official leader of the expedition I should go first. Rizzio, his heavy pistols drawn and ready, brought up the rear.

As caves go it was a nice enough cave. There wasn't any spectacular stalactites and stalagmites – neither were there hordes of swooping, squeaking bats or the like that one finds all too often. The floor was reasonably smooth, reasonably level. The sand still bore the imprint of the feet of Captain Spence and his party.

We found the first chamber with its paintings. We did not need to make a round of the walls prodding with an experimental forefinger. The paint was dry – and it was old.

We found the second chamber. There was, at the end of it, a half-finished painting. A flash bulb flared as Sarah photographed it. We waited until our eyes had recovered from the sudden glare, then looked at the picture by the light of our torches. It was not the same as the others. They showed men attacking animals – *this* depicted men attacking men.

Cautiously, I went forward, putting out my finger. It came away from the flat wall smeared with black and orange. I smelled it. There was the acrid tang of charcoal, the pungent stink of rancid animal fat.

'Sarah,' I said. 'Captain Spence was right. There *is* somebody painting in this cave. Can you *feel* anybody? Is it some half-crazed survivor of a shipwreck? Is it somebody who was left behind when the colony was evacuated?'

'Human . . .' she murmured, her eyes shut and a look of intense concentration on her face. 'Human – but not of

Earth. There's anger, and resentment, and it's closing in ...' Her eyes snapped open. 'Jim! Luigi! We'd better get out of here – and fast!'

Then we saw him.

He was standing there, glaring at us. He was human enough, if one discounted the furry, pointed ears. There was little about him of the ancestral ape. He was all of six feet tall and was slenderly built. The dark eyes in the thin dark face were intelligent. He wore a kilt of stinking, half-cured hide of some kind. His hands and forearms were spattered with the primitive pigments that he had been using. He looked at the smear on the wall that I had made. He looked at my stained hands.

'Tell him we're friends!' I said urgently to Sarah.

She said, 'I'm trying. He does not want to hear me. He's shutting me out.'

'If he starts anything ...' growled Luigi.

I turned to look at him. He was poised, tense, his heavy pistols ready. I hoped that the unarmed artist wouldn't start anything and wondered if I'd be able to stop Rizzio from doing him serious injury.

The caveman, still glaring at me, said something.

'He is angry with you,' said Sarah. 'Very angry.'

'Try and get the idea across that I apologise for smudging his painting,' I said.

'I *am* trying.'

What followed was, I know, quite inexcusable. Somehow the three of us, even Rizzio, were concentrating upon that one artist, trying to convey our apologies. We should have left it to our specialist, Sarah. Luigi should have been alert for other dangers. I, as coordinator, should have seen to it that each of the others was doing his or her own job. But, somehow, that spoiled painting was for all of us the most important thing in the Universe.

We were unprepared for what happened. We were taken by surprise by the volley of stones, flung with considerable force and accuracy from the shadows. Luigi cursed as his pistols were dashed from his hands. One of them went off, the noise of it in that confined space deafening. One stone hit my right wrist so that I dropped the torch, another caught me fairly in the belly. I heard Sarah scream as the light was smashed from her grasp. I was on the cave floor then, doubled up with agony and gasping for breath. I was aware of the scuffle going on around me and over me. Hard, naked feet kicked the breath from me – what little breath I had remaining after the initial blow. Something hit me violently on the side of the head and I lost consciousness.

Returning to my senses was a slow and painful process. The first thing of which I was aware was pain – pain in my head, pain all over my bruised body, pain at my wrists and ankles. I tried to raise my hands to my throbbing temples, found that they were tied. I opened my eyes slowly, was conscious of the flickering redness firelight.

Then I saw Sarah. She was lying not far from me. She was naked, and trussed, as I was trussed, with what looked like strips of hide. A dreadful fear came over me.

Before I could speak, she said, 'It's all right. These people don't find me at all attractive – they prefer their women much meatier. The only one who *might* be interested is the artist, but he'll have to have the Chief's permission first ...'

Rizzio, also naked, was just beyond her. He ignored us. He was glaring at the men sitting around the fire. They – squat, chunky savages – were pawing our clothing and possessions with interest. It was obvious, even to a non-telepath like myself, that the gunman regarded the alien hands on his precious firearms almost as a woman would regard her violation.

A little apart from the others sat the artist. He was more interested in us than in what we had worn, what we had carried. I thought with a chill of what Sarah had said, but I knew that, to him, the first thing of real importance was to depict us in imperishable paint on the eternal stone.

'If these people are cannibals,' I said bitterly, 'I wish that they'd eaten the Initial Survey Team!'

'You can say that again!' growled Luigi. 'When we get back – *if* we get back – I hope that you put in a stinking report!'

That 'if' coming from Luigi was rather shocking – but the loss of his guns had made him feel even more naked and helpless than Sarah and myself.

'Before you start blaming them,' said Sarah softly, 'just try to work things out ... Tell me, Jim, have you ever known an Initial Survey to miss a whole tribe of intelligent natives?'

'No. But there has to be a first time for everything.'

'Do you really think that they could have remained undetected when this world was colonised – an entire tribe ...?

'It seems doubtful, Sarah. But how else ...?'

'I', she said, 'am your specialist in certain matters. I'll tell you now that psychic emanations can be focused just as light can be focused – and that, obviously, is what has happened here. To work it out properly I'd have to be an astronomer, which I'm not – but it seems to me that this planet – although perhaps not all the time – gets the full force of the ... *fear* generated upon a dozen or so of the colonised Rim Worlds. It was that omnipresent dread that made the colonists here demand to be taken off.

'Now – what is that fear? It's a simple one – and a primitive one. Fear of the dark. It's a fear that we've inherited from our forebears, who lived lives very similar to those of these people. It's that intense fear that, beating on and around this planet, has pulled these people from their own time to ours ...'

'Which could,' I said slowly, 'account for the way in which they vanished. They vanished not in Space, but in Time ...'

'Then how was it that Captain Spence didn't see them, but found only the wet paint?' asked Rizzio, glad of something to take his mind off the way in which his precious weapons were being pawed by greasy, alien hands.

'I think I can account for that,' I said. 'He landed here, you remember, to recalibrate his Mannschenn Drive controls. The temporal fields generated by his Drive must have thrown the natives back to their own Time.'

'All very interesting,' he muttered, 'in an academic sort of way. But, as you reminded us, Sarah – you're the telepath. What's cooking?' He essayed a not at all funny jest. 'Will it be us?'

'I'm afraid so' she said. 'Unless ...'

'Unless what?' I asked sharply.

'There might be a way ...' she said slowly. 'After all, I'm an all-rounder – and that's part of the trouble. I can feel as those people feel. Those paintings of theirs, of course, have a certain magical significance. The artist depicts men hunting and killing animals – and thereby makes a spell to ensure that the hunt will be successful. *Somebody* – we know that it was Captain Spence and his crew – damaged the paintings and broke the spell. The cavemen knew from the evidence of footprints and such that it was human beings who were responsible – so the artist made more magic to bring the culprits to book. By all the laws of Absolute Ethics they're the injured parties.'

'Absolute tomfoolery!' snarled Rizzio.

He spoke too loudly.

One of the cavemen left the group by the fire, lurched

across to us and struck him heavily across the mouth. Rizzio spat blood and a broken tooth. If looks could have killed his eyes would have been far more deadly than his guns ever had been.

We were all of us silent for a while, listening to the meaningless chatter of the primitives. We watched as one of the men managed to insert his huge frame into Rizzio's blouse and shorts, listened to the laughter as the material split at the seams. I began to wonder what would happen when they became too curious about the firearms. There, just possibly, might lie our salvation. But they seemed to know, somehow, that the things were weapons and treated them with great respect.

I whispered, 'I can see your point, Sarah, although I don't agree with you. Surely, there must be a way ...'

She murmured, 'There is. You will see. Be ready for anything, both of you.'

My wrists were numb, and it was some time before I became aware of the odd sensation. Like a little snake, it was, slithering over my skin. My hands were tied behind me, and I could not see what was happening. I was afraid. I thought that it was a snake. I dare not move lest I infuriate the thing and cause it to use its poison fangs.

Then there was the same sensation at my ankles. There I could see what it was that was going on. Slowly, the crude knots in the strips of hide were coming untied. I looked at Sarah, saw from her rapt expression that she was concentrating hard, remembered that telekinesis was among her talents.

Slowly, circulation returned to feet and hands. It was painful in the extreme. Even so, I was able to see that Luigi was now free and that Sara's bonds were loosening themselves. I could tell that the gunman was tensing himself for a wild leap towards the heap of our possessions by the fire, that he hoped to be able to snatch his pistols and slaughter our captors.

'Don't!' I growled at him. '*Don't!*'

Some of the tension went out of him, but not much. 'Why not?' he demanded.

'Let Sarah play this hand.'

'Yes,' she said. 'Leave it to me.'

Once again we were making too much noise. Once again the same brute who had silenced us before left his seat by the fire, began to lurch towards us.

Suddenly there was a scream from the wall of the cave against which the women were huddled. Little tongues of flame had sprung up among the dried bracken which seemed to be their communal bed. A child ran from the group, her hair ablaze.

'*Damn!*' muttered Sarah. 'I didn't mean ...'

More flames were springing up – from our untidily piled clothing, from the hide aprons worn by the men. Our self-appointed guard yelled as he pulled his smouldering garment from him.

'*Now!*' shrieked Sarah.

Rizzio and I were on our feet at once. I pulled Sarah to hers. Rizzio sprang for the fire, pushing the astonished and panicking savages out of his way. Careless of burns, he snatched up his two point five automatics.

'Luigi!' Sarah was screaming. 'No. *No!* I promised ...'

The guns spoke, jumping in Rizzio's hands. I heard him cursing above the staccato, echoing thunder of the discharges. Even in the excitement and fear of the moment I could see that all his shots were going wild.

Rough hands grabbed my shoulder. I let go of Sarah, turned to fight off my attacker. It was the artist. He evaded that blow that I swung at him, caught Sarah by the wrist, began to drag her towards the exit of the chamber. I stumbled after them, became aware that Luigi was by my side. Behind us the fire had spread and a barrier of flame was, for the time being, at least, holding off pursuit and giving us enough light to see the way, enough light to see the pale form of the girl, the darker shape of her captor.

They had stopped running. The caveman was squatting on the sandy floor, his arms making strange, sweeping movements. Sarah stood beside him.

'I've still one round!' gasped Rizzio, raising his right hand to fire.

'Luigi!' Sarah's voice was peremptory. 'Put that thing down. At once!'

'But . . .'

'Better do as she says,' I told him.

'And watch where you're walking!' she ordered.

We approached the pair cautiously. The caveman, I saw, was drawing rapidly in the sand, sketching an outline with swift, sure strokes. With consummate artistry he suggested the hunger of the animal that he was drawing, its hunger and its viciousness. It didn't look the sort of beast that I'd want to meet on a dark night. It didn't look the sort of beast that I'd want to meet at high noon.

There was another tunnel running at right angles to the one that we were in. From it came an ominous snuffling sound, the scraping of sharp talons on rock. I looked at the primitive, yet vigorous, outline in the sand and visualised all too clearly the spiny, long-snouted, sharp-toothed thing that was coming towards us.

The artist whipped off his breech-clout, flung it back the way we had come. Then, catching Sarah's hand in his, he started to run. We followed. For the last part of the journey we were travelling blind and I wished that Luigi had had the sense to grab our torches rather than his guns. Such an experience is bad enough when you are fully clothed and stoutly shod. Luigi and I were torn and bleeding when we emerged into the open air at last. Sarah and the artist were almost unscathed.

The helicopter was still there. Somehow – although

we had to jettison some of our supplies – the cabin managed to hold all four of us. As we took off we heard an increasing uproar coming from the cavern and knew that the cavemen, not lacking in experience in dealing with the brute we had left to cover our escape, would almost certainly be victorious.

It was good to know that they wouldn't be able to reach us in our orbiting lifeboat.

It seemed a long time before *Lady Faraway*, in response to the calls put out by Sarah and Raul, flickered into sight to pick us up. It *was* a long time, subjectively. It was a long time, that is, for Luigi and myself. Luigi was mourning the loss of his confidence in his hitherto invincible guns and, so far as I know, has never forgiven Sarah for the telekinetic interference that had ruined his aim.

'But I promised Raul,' she told him. 'I promised him that when he helped us to escape I would not let you use your weapons on his people ...'

Luigi was mourning the loss of his marksman's confidence – and I was mourning the loss of Sarah.

'I still love you,' she said, 'in a way. But you're not a telepath, and you have no talent that could be trained and developed. Raul *is* is a telepath – and other things. Look at it this way – could *you* live with a woman with whom you had no common language? I can talk to Raul as I could never talk to you.'

'And you can love him as you never loved me,' I said bitterly.

'But of course. And I can love him as I never loved any of my fellow telepaths at the Institute. What attracted me to you was that you were a man of action. Raul is a man of action, too – *and* one of us.'

So *Lady Faraway* picked us up and carried us back to Thule. Raul adjusted amazingly both during that voyage and thereafter – but he was living in Sarah's mind and she was living in his, so perhaps it wasn't so amazing after all. He must have done more adjusting on the long voyage back to Earth, but regarding that I have no first-hand knowledge. I made sure that I didn't travel in the same ships.

He's the darling of the Rhine Institute now, which body is having the time of its collective life investigating the sympathetic magic that must have been used by Earth's cavemen-artists in the distant past. They don't know yet how a picture of an animal ever had the power to influence the animal itself, but they hope to find out. They are trying to find out, too, if Raul's last painting on Kinsolving, the one showing men attacking men, *did* pull Sarah and Luigi and myself all the way across the Galaxy to the Rim.

The Man Who Could Not Stop

They aren't particular about settlers in the Rim Worlds.

They can't afford to be. The night sky, at those seasons of the year when the sun is in conjunction with the great lens of the Galaxy, is frightening, even to those who were born and reared there, on the planets of the last, the ultimate frontier. It is the emptiness of the firmament that is so shocking, the emptiness made even worse by the dim, incredibly distant nebulosities that are the other galaxies, that are island universes. Many a man has come to Thule, or Faraway, or Ultimo to carve out a new career and, after a stay of only a few months, has taken ship for some planet in towards the Galactic centre, for some world where at night the sky is ablaze with stars, with beckoning, comradely lights of far-flung colonies and kingdoms.

There is a continual drain of population from the Rim Worlds. Their imports are, literally, everything, and their exports are young men and women. Without Federation aid the colonies would have to be abandoned; but they are lookout posts on the frontier of the endless dark, and as such must be maintained.

They are also the worlds from which a man on the run can run no further.

Clavering was on the run, and he ran to Faraway. Clavering was wanted, originally, on Earth, but during his flight he had contrived to make himself interesting to the police forces of at least a dozen other planets. His original crime had been robbery with violence – and what made it worse, from the viewpoint of the Terran authorities, was that the victims of the crime had been non-human, and highly important non-humans at that. It was unthinkable, of course, that the Shaara Empire should go to war with the Federation over the theft of the imperial regalia; even so, the High Queen cut short her visit to Washington and her farewell to Terran dignitaries was rather less than warm.

Clavering was on the run, and he bribed and hid and forged and stowed away, and somehow he stayed free and somehow kept moving. Plastic surgeons on four planets helped him with changes of identity. Somewhere along the line he added murder to his crimes – although it was really self defence; Clavering's spirit was restless, driving, self-torturing ... but it was not wholly evil. There were other thefts – mainly of money. The larger items of the High Queen's regalia, even when broken up, were not easy to dispose of.

He had known for a long time, as do all who live on the wrong side of the Law, that there is no extradition from the Rim Worlds. It was on Van Diemen's Planet that he made his decision. A friendly police officer had warned him, for a consideration, that Terran agents would be arriving on the next in-bound liner, and the tramp freighter *Jolly Swagman*, owned by the Faraway Line and homeward bound, was almost ready to blast off from Port Tasman. Her captain was ready and willing to supplement his salary by arranging a passage at very short notice.

It is a long run from Van Diemen's Planet to Faraway, all of twelve weeks, subjective time, and the queer, dimension warping fields of the Drive have time to build up so that the last half of the voyage is made through an utterly unreal continuum. Through the wide viewpoints are seen not the usual swirls of light, but star upon star, stretching, apparently, to infinity. Some captains making the run to the Rim warn their passengers what to expect when the Interstellar Drive is shut off. Others don't – and the Captain of *Jolly Swagman* was one of their number.

It was a shock like a physical blow – that sudden emptiness where, a split second before, all the hosts of heaven had blazed. The one lonely sun, and beyond it the few dim nebulosities, made it worse than complete emptiness would have been.

Clavering looked, and gulped, and decided that he would not like Faraway.

He did not revise his opinion when, two days later, he faced the Immigration officials at Port Remote. He had looked at the mirror in his cabin before going down to the ship's lounge, had decided that the very ordinary looking Mr Jones – face-shaped face, hair-coloured hair, eye-coloured eyes – bore no resemblance to the rather striking James Clavering who had run from Earth. He had checked his papers. They were good papers, as they should have been. He had certainly paid enough for them.

The senior immigration inspector sat at one of the lounge tables, the purser beside him. He looked up as Clavering approached, bleak, grey eyes belying the almost infantile chubbiness of his rosy face.

'This is Mr Jones,' said the Purser.

The inspector ignored him.

'Your name,' he said, 'is Clavering. You are wanted for robbery with violence on Earth, murder on Carribea, forgery on Nova Caledon ...'

'My name,' said Clavering, 'is Jones. I have papers ...'

'Of course you have. Who did you get 'em from, by the way? Lazarus on Nova Caledon, or Macdonald on Van Diemen's Planet?'

'My name,' repeated Clavering, 'is Jones.'

'Mr Jones,' said the inspector, 'I'm sure you know that there's no extradition here. But – and bear this in mind –

we can, in extreme cases, deport. Furthermore, we have an efficient police force and our prisons are not the luxury hotels that they are elsewhere in the Galaxy. As I expect you will learn. I hope I'm wrong – I rarely am.'

The bleak eyes moved on.

After his passport had been stamped Clavering said a few farewells aboard the ship, then took a taxi from the spaceport to Faraway City. The city was what he had expected it to be, a slightly overgrown town. Dwarfing it were the snow-capped mountains of the Last Range – named, as Clavering knew from his reading in the ship's library, after Commodore Last who had made the initial landing on Faraway.

He booked in at the hotel – Rimrock House – that had been recommended to him by the purser. After his baggage had been brought up he locked the door and made sure that what remained of the Shaara jewels was safe. Then he sat on the bed to think things over.

He had had plenty of time for reading on the voyage from Port Tasman. He had discovered that the laws of the Rim Worlds protected criminals from the consequences of crimes committed elsewhere in the Galaxy but, at the same time, were designed to rob them of the proceeds of such crimes. For example, he could take the Shaara High Queen's diamond-encrusted belt to any of the city jewellers without fear of arrest. *But* – the jeweller could take possession of it, turn it in and share in any reward money.

'They're a bunch of crooks,' Clavering growled.

There must, he thought, be fences on Faraway. The problem was how to find them. Another possible problem was that the news might already spread that Clavering, the man who stole the Shaara imperial regalia, was on Faraway. In which case Clavering could expect a visit from the local underworld.

Clavering inspected the contents of his wallet. His

Federation currency was legal tender, but he had enough only for a week's board and lodging. He looked at his watch, which he had adjusted to local time and length of day. It was mid-afternoon. By evening, he hoped, he would be well on his way to finding his feet in this new world.

The jewels he stowed in a large briefcase, which he chained and locked to his wrist. He had noticed, on the way in from the spaceport, that the building next door to the hotel was the First National Bank of Faraway, and his first move was to deposit the briefcase in the bank's strong-room.

He sauntered away from the bank, towards the centre of the city. There were, he noted approvingly, plenty of policemen, very smart and efficient looking in their neat uniforms of white shirt and blue kilt. He had already decided what crime he would commit; he did not think that shop-lifting would be a sufficiently heinous offence to merit deportation rather than jail. He hoped that the jails would not be as bad as the immigration inspector had implied.

He walked into a large store, took the escalator to the Men's Clothing department, sauntered casually along the aisles until he saw a display – of Altairan crystal silk belts – that took his fancy. He picked up one of the belts, admired the way that it clung to his hands in an almost sentient manner. With elaborate unconcern he rolled it up, slipped it into the inside pocket of his jacket. He walked slowly towards the *Down* escalator.

Five yards before he got to it, he felt a firm hand on his elbow ...

The magistrate before whom Clavering appeared was suitably censorious, with reference to abuse of the open-handed hospitality of Faraway. He regretted that the penalty of deportation did not apply to the crime of which Clavering had been found guilty. He passed sentence.

'Six months,' he said happily. 'Six months' hard labour.'

'But, Your Worship,' said Clavering. 'This is my first offence.'

'On this world, perhaps,' replied the magistrate. Then, to the policeman, 'Take him away.'

They took him away.

Clavering sat on his cot in the bare cell.

I'll have to make the best of it, he thought. *Six months is longer than I need to find the name of a reliable fence – but I should be able to find out plenty more. When I leave here I'll have all my contacts lined up. I'll know just how far I can go without getting deported . . .*

He stood up as the small shutter at the top of the door slammed open, and took the tray of food that was passed in to him. He looked at the soggy bread, the beans swimming in water gravy, the jug of water. He carried the tray to the cot, sat down and began to eat.

He passed out the tray when the shutter opened again. He lay down on the cot. He slept.

He slept surprisingly well. He was ready for his breakfast – although it was no more palatable than his supper had been – when it was passed in to him. When the door was unlocked, he joined a procession of shaven-headed figures in glaringly striped uniforms. The guards, he noted, were well armed and looked as though they would stand no nonsense. He sighed. This was his third spell in jail, but his two previous experiences had been in establishments where the accent was on humanitarianism.

The hard labour was something about which he had read in historical novels but which he had thought no longer existed. It was stone breaking in the prison quarry – monotonous, back-breaking toil. He had hoped to be able to engage in conversations with fellow inmates during the outdoor activity, but the noise of hammers crashing on rock and the vigilance of the guards made this almost impossible.

The little, wizened man on his right did manage to ask, out of the corner of his mouth, 'Are you a Rimmer?' and Clavering managed a hasty negative reply, and that was all.

The midday meal was eaten in the open – bread, beans and some unidentifiable meat that was all fat and gristle – but there were no opportunities for conversation. The afternoon passed in monotonous toil. Clavering was glad when he was locked in his cell for the night.

Six months. One hundred and eighty days. Do they work a seven day week? These damned guards must be recruited from a Trappist monastery, and they expect the rest of us to be Trappists, too ... At this rate I shall be no wiser when I come out than when I went in. Well, tomorrow I'm going to talk whether they like it or not. After all, they can't shoot me ...

Or can they?

The following day his resolve was unshaken. He noticed that the little, wizened man was walking ahead of him in the procession.

'You!' he said, in ordinary conversational tones. 'You! Shorty! Are you a Rimmer?'

The huge fist of the nearest guard drove, without warning, into his face. He staggered and fell. More intense than the pain was the feeling of consuming rage. He was on his feet again with a catlike agility, his own fists pounding into the bloated belly of the guard. Again he fell, this time under a rain of blows from behind. He was sufficiently in control of himself to roll into a ball, protecting his face with his arms from the heavy boots. It seemed far too long a time before he lost consciousness.

*

Gradually he became aware of a grey ceiling. He became aware, too, of pain - a dull ache over his legs and arms and most of his body, sharper pangs in his chest as he breathed. He turned his head so that the right side of his face lay on the pillow, groaning as the muscles of his neck protested. He could not, he discovered, see too well with his left eye. He saw a grey wall and the blurry figure of a man in convict stripes.

'Welcome back, Clavering,' said the man.

'Who're you?' Clavering grunted with an effort.

'I'm the Doctor. Doctor and inmate both. I'm too useful to them ever to be turned loose. Besides, I know to much ... Here, drink this!'

Clavering managed to struggle to a half-sitting position in the bed. He brought his good eye to bear on the doctor, saw an old man with scanty white hair, a deeply lined, grey face. With an effort he took the glass from him.

It was good brandy, even though it did cause the lacerations inside his mouth to sting painfully. After a few seconds Clavering felt stronger. He looked down at his body, from which the sheet had fallen, saw the taped ribs, the huge, blotchy bruises.

He said, without passion, 'The bastards.'

'You asked for it,' said the doctor. 'You asked for it, and you got it. I'd have thought that a man with your wide experience would have had more sense than to behave the way you did. I'd have thought that a man with your experience would have had more sense than to have landed in this hell hole in the first place.'

'There were reasons,' said Clavering.

'There always are,' said the old man. 'But go on.'

'Can I trust you?' asked Clavering.

'Everybody trusts me - even the guards, even the Governor. They have to.'

'Why don't they release you?'

'There's a limit to their trust. Besides . . . Do you know, I've no desire to get out into the world again. In many ways I have more freedom here than outside. Of course, I can't dress as I please – but, in compensation, I have no tailor's bills.'

'All right,' said Clavering abruptly. 'I can trust you. But is this place bugged? It seems to be the one spot where a man can talk . . .'

'This isn't what you'd call a modern jail,' said the doctor. 'As you've found out for yourself. None of *them* would ever have the intelligence to plant microphones.'

As he spoke, he was scribbling on a pad. He held it so that Clavering could see the crabbed writing.

Of course, it's bugged. But carry on talking. Use the pad for anything important.

'I've a little money,' said Clavering. 'Or I had. It was in my wallet in my jacket pocket. I suppose it's in the Governor's safe now . . .'

He wrote: *I'm a stranger here – I thought jail would be the best place to make contacts . . .*

It may still be there, if you're very lucky,' said the doctor.

What I want, wrote Clavering, *is the name of a good fence.*

He said, 'I was hoping that you might be able to get the money out for me. On other worlds prisoners can arrange to buy stuff from the outside – this jail diet needs some help.'

'On other worlds,' said the doctor, 'they pamper their convicts.'

He wrote: *I can hear them coming. I must flush these pages away.*

'After all,' said Clavering to the retreating back, 'we are human beings.'

'Are we?' asked the doctor. There was the sound of running water. 'Are we?'

'A pig couldn't stomach the muck they feed us here,' said Clavering.

A door opened. A tall man in plain black clothing walked in, escorted by two uniformed guards. He nodded curtly to the old doctor, who replied with a nod of equal curtness. He stood by Clavering's bed, looking coldly down on him.

Clavering returned the stare. He wondered, as he had wondered when he had first met the Governor in his office, what an ex-spaceman was doing in such a position. In the other jails that he had known, the Governors had been either retired military men or high ranking police officers.

'No permanent damage, I trust?' said the Governor to the doctor.

'No thanks to your bullies. But he'll live.'

'This,' said the Governor to Clavering, 'is not a Rest Home. On this world, on any of the Rim Worlds, we do not believe in pampering criminals. Criminals may come here, as you have done, to avoid the consequences of their crimes elsewhere in the Galaxy. If they make good citizens they are welcome. If they don't ...'

'I'm beginning to regret having come here,' said Clavering through swollen lips.

'No doubt you are. No doubt you have become used to being treated as a hospital patient rather than as a convict, as an interesting case to be studied by gentle and considerate psychiatrists. Here, on Faraway, we recognise only one school of psychology.'

'Which is?' asked Clavering, feeling that it was expected of him.

'Pavlov's,' replied the Governor.

'It is hard,' said the doctor, 'to build up a conditioned reflex against wrongdoing in an adult human being.'

'We can try,' said the Governor.

*

At last, with no remission for good conduct, the six months were over. Clavering had his last interview with the Governor, handed in his prison uniform and received in exchange his civilian clothing, found that his watch, his wallet and his money were missing. His protests were laughed at.

He was met at the gate of the jail by a ground car with *Prisoners' Aid Society* emblazoned on its sides in huge white letters. He had no option but to accept the proffered help. He rode back to Faraway City seated beside the driver, a huge man who, to judge by his appearance, was an ex-policeman. Poverty, thought Clavering, makes strange bedfellows.

On the outskirts of the city they pulled up alongside a drab, barracks-like building which obviously – its occupants being lavish in their use of neon signs – was the headquarters of the Society. The driver of the car took Clavering into the office where a repellently fat woman took down his particulars. He was then told that the Society would find him work and would house and feed him – his board and lodging beind deducted by his employer from his weekly pay – until such time as he could fend for himself. A job, it appeared, was already waiting for him – one of the firms of importers had a vacancy for a junior clerk. He was to start the following morning.

Clavering thanked the woman with more politeness than sincerity, was led by a skinny girl to a sparsely furnished cubicle. The girl turned to leave.

'Wait!' said Clavering. 'Please ...'

The girl said sullenly, 'Old blubber-guts will throw a fit if I'm not back in the office in two seconds flat.'

'Let her,' said Clavering. 'What's the set-up here?'

'You make your own bed and sweep your own floor,' said the girl. 'You eat at o-seven-thirty and eighteen hundred hours. On Saturdays and Sundays the hostel gives you a noon meal too. It ain't any good.'

'What I meant was – what are the chances of getting out of here?'

She laughed. 'None. By the time the cost of your board and lodging have been taken out of your pay you'll have enough left for a couple of shots and a deck of smokes. And with your record you won't get a job anywhere except through the Society.'

'This,' said Clavering, 'is worse than jails I've been in on more civilised planets.'

'Nobody,' she pointed out, 'asked you to come here.'

She left him. Clavering went to the blotchy mirror, looked at himself. His suit was still a fair fit, although it tended to be a little tight cross the chest and shoulders, more than a little slack across the belly. Clavering shrugged. It didn't much matter. He would soon have money enough – even though the fence in Faraway City would be no more honest than fences are anywhere – to buy a new suit, to set himself up in some sort of business.

In some sort of business? He asked himself with a certain amazement. What's come over me? Was Pavlov right after all? But I don't want to risk another spell in that jail . . .

He left the hostel.

He had no money, so he had to walk to the city, feeling thankful that it was no more than an overgrown town. He went first to Rimrock House, and found that his baggage had been stored and that there were storage charges to pay. He said that he would pick it up later.

He went into the First National Bank. The official in charge of safe deposits remembered Mr Jones. Even so, there were certain formalities to be observed – fingerprint and retinal patterns to check, five months' storage charges to pay . . . He was sorry, but rules were made for the protection of customers as well as for the protection of the bank and, furthermore, were not made to be broken . . .

Clavering left the bank. It was past noon, and he had had nothing to eat since his prison breakfast. He hadn't had a drink for six months, and had had nothing to smoke in that period but the vile, acrid prison tobacco.

He considered walking to the address that the doctor had given him, but it was on the other side of the city and there was, too, the possibility that the fence would refuse to advance him the money for his immediate requirements. Anyhow, Clavering had his pride, and he didn't like fences, and hated to place himself under any obligation to one.

It was lucky, thought Clavering, that he had never become a specialist. He could crack a safe or forge a signature or pick a pocket – not, of course, with the best practitioners of these various arts but with, he prided himself, the second best. The present situation called for a pocket picking. He began to look around him for a likely mark.

A prosperous-looking fat man was window shopping nearby. Clavering ran a trained eye over his clothing. The shirt was Altairan crystal silk, and Altairan crystal silk is not among the cheaper textiles. The jacket was one of the finer, more expensive tweeds from Nova Caledon, and the kilt and stockings obviously came from Scotland itself. (Clavering wondered if the fat man had any right to wear the Clan Graeme tartan.) The shoes had that sheen peculiar to leather made from the hides of the great fish lizards of the Markara swamps. The bulge under the jacket was almost certainly a well-filled wallet.

Clavering waited until the fat man was staring into the window of a delicatessen, well stocked with gastronomical temptation from a score of worlds, before making his approach. He sauntered up to him and said, 'Pardon me, have you the time? My watch is being repaired . . .'

'Twelve after thirteen,' replied the other, affably enough.

'Quite a fine display, isn't it?' said Clavering, nodding towards the window. 'Of course some of these things don't travel too well. The only way to eat witchety grubs, for example, is to pick them straight from the hot ashes on to which they've been dropped alive and squirming ...'

'I've never been to Earth,' said the fat man. 'Next year, perhaps. But I always say that I can have a cruise of the Galaxy whenever I feel like it, in my own kitchen.'

'What's that stuff there?' asked Clavering. 'That opalescent jelly in the fancy jar?'

'It comes from Windhover. Have you ever been there?'

'No.'

'Neither have I – but, thanks to my hobby, I know plenty about it. At certain seasons of the year – and seasons there are rather complicated, as they're bound to be in a binary system – the big sea spiders come ashore and build nests among the rocks with secretions from their bodies ...'

When he had heard enough to make him resolve that no foodstuff from Windhover would ever find its way on to his table, Clavering asked the time again. He excused himself, saying that he had an appointment. He walked away – not too fast and not too slow, putting several corners between himself and the fat man. He arrived eventually in a small park. He found a vacant seat – the day was fine and warm and most of the office workers there were eating their lunches on the grass.

He pulled his prize, the precious wallet, out of his pocket.

It wasn't a wallet.

It was a cigar case.

Anyhow, thought Clavering, he would have a quiet smoke before doing anything further. He took one of the fat cigars, held it appreciatively under his nose, then lit it with the lighter that was part of the case.

It tasted ... odd.

It wasn't unpleasant, it was, most definitely, *good.* Its oddness was probably the result of having his palate ruined by the chopped straw and horse droppings that went by the name of tobacco in the Central Jail.

Horse droppings?

Insult to horse – man's best friend.

Without horses – what to bet on?

Dogs?

Hell with dogs!

Hate dogs.

One there, taking fat woman for walk.

Coming this way.

Hell wif'm.

Going to kick me.

Kick'm first.

Madam, I refuse to be kicked by your mangy cur. I have refused to be kicked by mangy curs on every civilised planet of Galaxy. Matter of principle, tha's wha'. Man of principle, tha' me.

'Scuse ... Not well ... Must be fish or something ...

It was not the fish, fish being a luxury of which Clavering had not partaken for months. It was the cigar. It was a very expensive cigar – being rolled from a mixture of Terran tobacco and the Lyran *kaleph* weed. The fumes from their joint burning produce an effect very like that of alcohol, and when taken on an empty stomach and after half a year of abstinence from strong drink, intoxication is the inevitable result.

The magistrate before whom Clavering appeared on his drunk and disorderly charge greeted him as an old enemy. He repeated his remarks about the abuse of Rim World hospitality. He even went so far as to repeat the sentence. The sentence might have been less had it not been discovered that the cigar case did not bear Clavering's name.

He was in a bitter mood when he was taken to the Central Jail.

He stood sullenly before the Governor.

'I thought,' said that official, 'that you would be a repeater, but I did not expect you back so soon.'

'I did not expect to be back at all.'

'But you are,' said the Governor tiredly. 'However, I have decided to be lenient. You are a man of intelligence, and that intelligence is wasted on the rock pile. We have, strange though it may seem, some machinery in this establishment, and it has to be maintained ...'

'And will the better job bring better food?' asked Clavering bluntly.

'The food will be the same. Really it should be inferior, as you will be expending far less physical energy.'

'Sir,' said Clavering earnestly, 'may I ask you a question?'

'You may.'

'Then tell me – just what crime must one commit to get oneself deported from the Rim Worlds?'

'Not murder,' replied the Governor, smiling bleakly. 'We hang people for that. We're very old fashioned here, as you may have noticed. As a matter of fact three convictions running, for any crime or crimes, is usually sufficient. That's the law.'

'Thank you,' said Clavering.

His second sentence dragged as slowly as his first one had.

This time he managed to avoid any serious physical maltreatment and his only visit to the hospital was when he was suffering from a slightly infected hand. Guards were present while it was being dressed and he was unable to tell his story to the old doctor.

The time dragged – yet, in spite of himself, he found himself developing a very real interest in machinery.

When at last the day came for him to leave the prison he had to fight down the feeling that he should say goodbye to his old, well polished, smoothly working charges.

The same ground car took him to Faraway City, the same fat woman admitted him to the Prisoners' Aid Society Hostel. He found as before, that there was a job waiting for him, but this time it was in one of the smaller garages in the city.

Clavering decided not to rush things this time. He did not go near either the hotel or the bank on his first day of freedom, but stayed in the hostel, reading. The following morning he reported for work in the garage and spent the forenoon cleaning and polishing one ground car and two helicopters. The boss advanced him enough money for his lunch, which he bought at a snack bar close to the garage. In the afternoon he was allowed, under supervision, to overhaul an engine.

He had his evening meal at the hostel. It was not much of an improvement over the prison food. When it had settled, he decided to walk to the address that he had been given during his first spell in jail.

It was a clear night, and it was the first time that Clavering had seen the night sky for a year. It was autumn in Faraway's northern hemisphere, and the Galactic lens was almost in conjunction with the sun. As Clavering walked slowly out along the road with its sparse lining of houses he looked upwards. The emptiness that he saw was as shocking as it had been the first time that he had seen it from *Jolly Swagman's* observation lounge. He understood now the stories he had heard to the effect that everybody who could afford to leave Faraway finished up in the Cluster Planets.

He reached, at last, the house where he had been told that he would find the fence. He hesitated for a while at the gate to the long drive, feeling an unwonted nervousness. What, he wondered, would go wrong this time? And the worst of it was that there was no place to run if things did go wrong. He had been running all his life and had come at the last to the very edge of the dark, the frontier of utter negation.

He shrugged.

These crazy Rim Worlds, he told himself, did things to you.

He pressed the button set in one of the posts of the wrought iron gate. There was a faint whirring sound that told him he was being scanned. From a hidden speaker came a metallic voice.

'Who are you? What do you want?'

'I am John Clavering. I wish to speak with your master, with Mr Konradis.'

'What is your business?'

'I will tell that to Mr Konradis.'

'I repeat: what is your business?'

'Damn nosy robot . . . My business is private.'

A new voice broke in, a human voice.

'What do you want?'

'Are you Mr Konradis?'

'Yes.'

'Then my business concerns the Shaara imperial regalia.'

There was a sharp intake of breath, distinctly audible to Clavering. There was a click as the lock of the gate was released. It swung silently open.

Clavering walked slowly up the drive, his boots crunching on the yellow gravel. He looked at the house that was more of a fortress than a dwelling place. The front door opened at his approach. Clavering stepped into a hall – bare, unfurnished, ablaze with harsh, blue-white light.

'Take the door to your right,' ordered a voice.

Clavering did so. He found himself in a room that was as large as the one that he had just left but, if anything, over-furnished, over-decorated. Behind a huge, polished desk sat a little man, the lamp light reflected gleamingly from his bald skull.

He said, 'Sit, Mr Clavering.'

Clavering sat.

He said, 'I suppose you have come to see if I wish to take the Shaara jewels off your hands.'

Clavering said yes.

'I will be honest with you, Mr Clavering. I will let you have five per cent of the value of the jewels. After all, if it had not been for you I should never have been able to engage in one of the more profitable deals in my career.'

'Five per cent! I promise you I will drop them in the sea before I will sell them for five per cent.'

'Mr Clavering, almost six months ago I was approached by the Queen-Captain of a Shaara vessel, and, much as I dislike dealing with non-humans, the arthropoda especially, I let her persuade me to use what little influence I have to recover the regalia from the bank.'

He paused. He put both hands into the drawer under the desk top. His right hand came up holding a bundle of banknotes, his left hand grasping a deadly little Minetti automatic. He said. 'Don't get ideas, Mr Clavering. I am left-handed. Catch!'

Clavering caught the money. He counted it. It would be enough to buy him a new suit and perhaps a used ground car or helicopter. It would not be enough to buy passage to another planet, even to one of the other Rim Worlds.

He said, 'The Shaara captain wasn't very generous.'

'She gave me all the Federation money she had in her ship's safe,' said Konradis.

'So there is more to come,' said Clavering.

'Maybe. But there is no more for you.'

Clavering choked down his rage. He put the money in

an inside pocket. He got to his feet, walked slowly to the door. The muzzle of the little automatic in Konradis's hand swung to follow him as he walked. Clavering ignored it. His photographic memory was hard at work, noting and filing details of windows and their fastenings, doors and their locks. He had met men of the receiver's type before and knew that they relied far more heavily upon robot guards than upon fallible humans.

He knew, as Konradis obviously didn't, that robots can be fallible too.

He left the house, left the grounds, walked slowly back to the city.

Back in the hostel Clavering went into his cubicle, lay on the bed and marshalled facts.

(a) What remained of the Shaara regalia when he had come to Faraway was by this time once again in the possession of the High Queen.

(b) Twenty times Cr. 1,000, which was what Konradis had given him, was Cr. 20,000. The fence must have made at least five times that amount on the deal, to judge by the reward that had been advertised after the theft had taken place.

(c) A passage to, say, Van Diemen's Planet would cost at least Cr. 2,500.

(d) A man like Konradis almost always kept a large sum of ready money in the house, usually in a bedroom safe.

(e) The doorkeeping robot was a Farrar-Blenkinsop, model Mark IV. Clavering knew things about the Mark IV, expertly extracted from a drunken Farrar-Blenkinsop technician.

(f) Konradis undoubtedly had friends on the police force, therefore his mouth must be shut for at least six hours after the burglary. There was a little somno gun in Clavering's baggage which would take care of that angle.

(g) Clavering's baggage was, presumably, still in the

Rimrock House storage rooms – but the Cr. 1,000 he had received from Konradis would be more than enough to cover the charges.

(h) Clavering's papers, made out in the name of Jones, were still in his baggage. A few Cr. 10 bills, wisely used, would get them stamped in the right places by the right people.

(i) The Interstellar Transport Commission's *Delta Serpens* was standing at Port Remote, scheduled to blast off for Mitylene at 2400 hours the following night ...

'So,' said Clavering to himself, 'if I catch her I run the slight risk of winding up in a Terran jail. It's only a slight risk – and, after all, Terran jails are luxury hotels compared with the one here. In any case, the Shaara High Queen's got her tomfoolery back by now so the heat must be off.

'If I stay here, I shall almost certainly wind up in jail again. Then I shall be deported. And that way it is *certain* that the police, local as well as Federal, will be waiting for me on whatever planet I'm sent to.

'It's worth the risk.'

He undressed, got into bed. Within seconds he was sleeping like a happy child.

The following morning he rang the garage, said that he was ill and would not be coming to work. He went straight to Rimrock House, where he had to wait for his baggage to be brought up from the storerooms. He took a taxi back to the hostel, took his baggage up to his room, locked the door and unpacked. He checked the little somno gun, testing it on one of the tiny flying lizards that were common pests on Faraway. It worked. He found the sheet of specially treated paper. Lacking infra-red scanning equipment he couldn't test that, but he had no reason to doubt that it would work. He repacked his baggage, putting all his papers in his briefcase, the somno gun in the side pocket of his kilt, the sheet of paper in the inside breast pocket of his jacket.

He went back to the job at the garage for what was left of the forenoon and all the afternoon. During the lunch break – he was left in charge while the other employees went out for their meal – he was able to take a good wax impression of the key to the main door. He decided which car he would use – a big, old-fashioned Ferranti monowheel.

He finished his day's work and returned to the hostel. Back in his cubicle he found signs that his baggage had been tampered with. The maid? The superintendent? One of the other ex-convict guests? It didn't matter. He was relieved to find that his tools and key blanks had not been stolen; replacements could be purchased easily in any hardware store, but all the shops were now shut until the following morning.

After dinner downstairs, he returned to his room. Behind the locked door he worked on one of his blanks, whistling to cover the rasping of his file.

When he was finished, he put the key and one of the files in his kilt pocker, and his papers into his briefcase. Into a small suitcase he packed bare necessities – the Delta-class liners, he knew, ran to a small ship's shop where he would be able to purchase anything further required during the voyage.

Carrying the two cases he went downstairs. He met only the skinny maid. She looked at him curiously.

He said, 'I should be able to get a fair price for these. I was talking to one of our customers in the garage today and he said he wanted to buy some good, secondhand baggage. I'm taking them out to him.'

She said, not really interested, that she hoped he got a good price.

He walked slowly into the city, to the office of the Interstellar Transport Commission's agents. It was still open, and would remain open until *Delta Serpens* had blasted off.

To the bored young man behind the counter Clavering said, 'Are there any berths left aboard the Earth ship?'

'Yes, sir. Not the best – they're all taken. There's a cabin on F level if you don't mind the heat and the noise.'

'I'll take it.'

'To Mitylene, or beyond?'

'What's the fare to Mitylene?'

'Two thousand.'

'I haven't that much with me right now,' said Clavering. 'I have to collect the balance from a friend this evening.'

'Two thousand,' said the clerk.

'It's rather important that I catch the ship,' said Clavering. 'I'm willing to make it worth your while. Suppose I make a deposit of Cr. 500 on my ticket ... Suppose I leave my papers with you, and this suitcase... You could get the papers fixed up for me, and I meet you at the spaceport at, say, 2330 hours. You give me my ticket, and I give you the balance of Cr. 2,500 ...'

This was the sort of arithmetic that the clerk understood.

He looked at the papers, riffled through them, and nodded.

'Yes, Mr Jones,' he said. 'It can be arranged. I'm sure that it can be arranged.'

Clavering paid out the initial five hundred credits, walked briskly out of the office. He looked up and down the street, his lip lifting in a sneer. A hick town on a hick planet. He looked up at the black, empty sky, thought how good it would be when he saw the great, blazing lens of the Galaxy fill *Delta Serpens'* viewpoints as she swung round to the course that would take her to Mitylene and to the thriving bustling worlds of the Inner Systems.

Clavering looked at his watch. He had time to kill. He

went into a Newsreel Theatre, watched events that were history rather than news. When he found himself watching, for a second time, the coronation of King James XIV of Waverley he left.

He strolled casually from the theatre to the garage. There were only a few passers-by, and there were no policemen in sight.

His new key was a good fit, opening the big doors with no delay. The big Ferranti was where he had left it, near the door. The gyroscope reached maximum revolutions inside three minutes and Clavering retracted the parking props, rolled slowly out into the street. He left the car briefly while he shut and locked the garage doors.

He made the run to Konradis' house without incident. He stopped the car just short of the ornamental gates and got out, leaving the gyroscope running. He started as a sudden, raucous sound broke the silence. So Konradis kept fowls, and one of his roosters had an odd sense of time ... He remembered the night that he had got Fredericks, the Farrar-Blenkinsop roboticist, drunk.

'Thing to 'member,' Fredericks had said, 'is this. All our robots have brains. But not human brains. Not anything like. Take Mark IV. Same IQ as domestic fowl ... Funny thing – bunch of us talking 'bout it, 'membered 'bout hypnotisin' chickens. Fantastic. Works on Mark IV too ...'

'And how do you hypnotise a chicken?' Clavering had asked.

'Easy. Draw line on floor. Hold her beak down to it.'

'But the Mark IV hasn't got a beak ...'

'Special paper, hold up to scanner. Shows, in infra-red, very straight, very dark line ...'

So Clavering had carried out his own experiments, but had been careful never to carry out a robbery by making use of the doorkeeping robot's weakness. He had decided to keep the knowledge in reserve until such time as its use would be justified.

This was the time.

He saw, on the nearer gatepost, the dim glow of the button. He took the specially prepared paper out of his pocket, unfolded it. He stood before the gatepost, the paper held over his face. With his right forefinger he found the button, pressed it. He heard the whirring noise as the scanner went into action.

'Who are you?' asked the metallic voice, then stopped.

'You know me,' said Clavering.

'Yes.'

'I am a friend.'

'Yes.'

'Let me in.'

'Yes.'

The lock clicked, the gate swung open. Clavering got back into the car – he would need it both as a means of transportation and as a temporary prison for Konradis – and drove up the drive. At his approach the front door of the house opened. He transferred the somno gun to the side pocket of his jacket. He got out of the car, walked to the door, into the house.

The muzzle of the gun was trained on the door to Konradis' study. As it opened. Clavering fired. He felt rather than heard the whine of the thing. He saw Konradis stagger inside the doorway, the automatic dropping from his hand. He saw Konradis fall, not unconscious, only partially paralysed.

Clavering dragged him into the study, propped him up in one of the chairs.

'I could have used full power,' said the thief, 'but I didn't. You're no use to me asleep. I want you to talk.'

'I ...' the words came with painful slowness, '... refuse.'

'Where is your safe?'

Konradis was silent.

'The trouble with somno guns,' remarked Clavering, 'is that the victim is quite insensitive to pain, so more extreme measures are required than would be the case otherwise.' He unbuckled Konradis' right shoe, pulled it off. He pulled off the stocking. 'You will be able to feel nothing, but you will be able to watch me build a fire in that ornamental but doubtless quite efficient fireplace of yours ... You have kindling and coals all ready – thoughtful of you. You will, as I have said, feel nothing – but it will be a rather trying experience for you to watch your foot being slowly consumed by the flames.'

'You ... daren't,' said Konradis.

'Daren't I?' asked Clavering, lighting the fire.

'Bedroom,' said Konradis when his foot was an inch from the fire. 'Behind ... picture ...'

'And the combination? Hurry, now – I might get tired and drop this foot.'

Konradis told him. Konradis told him too, reluctantly, of the concealed switch that would start the pump to evacuate the anaesthetic gas from the safe – this was after Clavering had placed a short stub of ornamental candle from the dining room in a box of highly inflammable material, telling Konradis that unless he was down from the bedroom in a reasonably short time he, Konradis, would suffer at least very severe burns before the fire extinguishing equipment came into action.

Clavering found the bedroom, and wished that he could have stolen its furniture and decorations – he had a sound, professional knowledge of antiques. He found the safe behind a genuine Picasso. He found the switch for the pump, concealed in the right nipple of a platinum nude by Kirschwasser. He waited until the whining of the little machine had stopped before he opened the safe.

There was currency – good, honest, Federation currency – ample for all his needs. Clavering stuffed it into a silken pillowslip from the bed. He went downstairs, blew out the candle under Konradis's chair.

'Now,' he said, 'you're coming with me.'

'Why?'

'Because I say so. The effects of a somno gun last only so long, and as soon as they wear off you'll be giving the alarm. If I tie you up and leave you here you might wriggle free. In the boot of the car you'll be quite safe – all that I have to do is give you an occasional jolt. Actually, I'm being very considerate.'

And, he thought, I can afford to be. I haven't lost the old touch. Tonight's operation went like clockwork.

It would have continued to go like clockwork had it not been for a drunken driver roaring out of a side street at excessive speed. The boot of Clavering's car was burst open in the crash and the police officer who was on the spot before Clavering could collect his scattered senses regarded its contents with interest.

Clavering would have used his somno gun, but the little weapon had been broken in the accident. Clavering grabbed his briefcase, into which he had transferred the stolen money, and tried to run. He was brought down by a flying tackle from a meddling passer-by.

The Governor looked across his desk at Clavering almost with approval.

'You're back,' he said.

'I'm back,' admitted the prisoner. 'How soon are they going to deport me? And where to?'

'Not so fast, Clavering. Not so fast. There is still the prison sentence to be served. We have some new machinery for you to look after – the pumps for our experimental hydroponics farm. We intend to make sure that you're well trained for your new life.'

'Very decent of you, I'm sure.'

'Oh, another point, Clavering – and your observance of it will save you a deal of trouble in the future. Just call me 'sir', will you?'

'All right,' said Clavering. 'Sir.'

He found his new work interesting. He found, too, that conditions were a lot easier, that the food was better and that the guards did not go to such extreme lengths to discourage conversation among the prisoners.

He soon realised that his workmates were men like himself, intelligent, but habitual criminals, incurable except by the personality-destroying brain surgery abhorred by all civilised worlds. He asked questions, but none of them knew to which planet or planets they were to be deported, or when. He discovered that a large number of convicts were being trained in other branches of engineering.

Then, at last, he was aroused one morning by the guard hammering at his door. He got up, began groping for his clothes. 'Not those,' barked the official. 'Put these on!' He thrust a bundle through the open trap.

There was underwear, clean and new. There was a black coverall. There was a pair of highly polished black boots. On each sleeve of the coverall was a green fern leaf superimposed upon a golden gear wheel.

The new clothing was comfortable, and it fitted. Clavering left his cell when the door was unlocked, joined a procession of similarly garbed prisoners. At the prison gates, where the vans were waiting, he stopped to ask one of the guards, 'What's wrong with the Governor? He usually says goodbye to his departing guests.'

'You'll be seeing Captain Christopher again,' said the guard.

Clavering could see nothing from inside the van, but he was not surprised when the door opened to reveal the environs of the spaceport. He looked with interest at the other vans that were drawn up in an orderly line, at the black-clad men who were tumbling out of each one. It was cheaper, he supposed, to arrange a mass deportation every so often.

He stiffened with surprise as he turned to look at the ship. She was big, far bigger than any vessel that he had ever seen. She dwarfed the spaceport administration buildings, the cranes and gantries. Her tail fins were flying buttresses and she was a huge, improbable tower built of gleaming metal.

'We're travelling in style,' said the man on Clavering's left. 'They've sent an Alpha-class liner to pick us up.'

'That's no Alpha-class liner,' said Clavering. 'It's at least twice that size!'

A voice was booming from loudspeakers: 'Attention, all! Attention, all! Personnel will board the ship forthwith!'

The long lines of men shuffled forward, with alert guards in close attendance as they passed up the ramps into the airlocks. There was an elderly man, in purser's uniform, on duty at the head of the ramp by which Clavering boarded. He was ticking off names on a sheet.

'Clavering, John – Hydroponics.'

The insignia on Clavering's sleeves, the work that he had been doing during his last prison sentence, added up to make sense.

'Making us work our passages?' he remarked.

The purser ignored him.

'Cowden, Peter – Air Circulation . . . Davis, David – Air Circulation . . .'

'Hydroponics men, this way!' a voice was shouting.

Clavering, with the other men of his department, followed the Master at Arms through alleyways and up ladders, found himself with eleven more deportees in a sparsely furnished dormitory. The petty officer ignored all questions. The steel door shut with a decisive click.

The time dragged. The men talked in a desultory way. They were grateful when the wall speaker came to life and ordered them to their bunks for blast-off. They resented not being told what was happening – all their past experience of space travel had been as fare-paying passengers. They were relieved when the thunders died and the crushing weight was lifted from their chests. There was a little horseplay as they tumbled about the compartment in free fall.

'Attention!' barked the wall speaker. The bulkhead below it had come alive, had become a huge video screen. It depicted what was obviously the control room of a spaceship. It showed a tall man in black uniform who wore on his sleeves the four gold bands of captaincy.

'The Governor!' whispered somebody. 'I thought he was just an ex-captain!'

'And there's the old Quack with him!' muttered one of the other men.

'Men,' said Captain Christopher quietly. 'I do you the honour of calling you men, because it is a man's job that lies before you. A job so dangerous and uncertain that free men who are willing to do it are hard to find ...

'History,' he said after a pause, 'repeats itself. Centuries ago there was another Christopher - although that was his given name - who knew that the Earth was round, and this in an age when the majority of seamen feared that if they sailed too far to the westward their ships, and themselves with them, would fall over the edge. This other Christopher, this Christopher Columbus, found that he could sail his ships only by impressing men from the jails.

'All of you who have come to the Rim Worlds have had your chances. All of you discovered, with your first experience of jail, that crime does not pay. And yet, although you knew that the penalty for habitual crime was deportation, you persisted in your ways. You are here, all of you, as the direct consequence of your own actions. The rest of us - myself, the officers and the petty officers - are here because we want to be. And I wish to make it clear that we do not intend to be thwarted in our purpose. I wish to make it clear that we, the professional spacemen, will be able to work the ship after a fashion should you be so unwise as to stage a mutiny. I wish to make it clear that under my command the rule is: He who does not work does not eat.

'I cannot say how long our voyage will take in terms of objective time – this is one of the things we have to find out. I cannot say, even, how long it will take measured by subjective time – but I think that we shall return before much more than a half century has passed.

'This I can say – there is no turning back. None of you knows enough to handle a spaceship. You might, in time, learn enough so that you think you will be able to seize the ship and force my navigators and engineers to do your bidding. I will tell you that the ship has defences built-in with such an emergency in mind. In the extremely unlikely event of a successful mutiny there will be, I promise you, no return ...'

Frantically, Clavering racked his mind for some legality in the name of which he could protest. There was none. By running to the Rim Worlds he had made himself subject to their laws, and one of those laws made deportation the punishment for the third conviction. He could not help but admire the cunning of the Federation – to make the Rim the haven for the criminal and to offer the criminal, on paper at least, the chance of reformation. It seemed that all who were potential space-crew material were given very little chance to reform.

With the others he watched as the control room scanner swung away from the Captain and his officers, watched as it showed that part of Space towards which the ship was heading. He heard the unique whine of a Mannschenn Drive starting up, knew that the screen would, in a few seconds, show only meaningless whorls of light.

And they would be better than the cold emptiness – the infinite nothingness interrupted only by the dim, distant nebulosity to which the ship was headed – the tiny, luminous cloud that was, perhaps, another Galaxy.

He had spent his life running, and he had run as far as he could, to the very edge of the night.

And he had not been able to stop.

The Key

There's a key.

Man has been hunting ever since Man *was* Man. That curiosity, I suppose, is a trait inherited from our simian ancestors. Had our forebears been of canine or of feline stock it is probable that we should not be spending so much of our time asking, *Why?* Dogs and cats are not of an enquiring nature, unless food is involved. Monkeys are. But if our ancestors had been dogs or cats we should not be Men, not in the true sense of the word, and our intellectual energies would be directed only towards the more efficient production of food and shelter, and it is highly probable that we should never have left the surface of our own planet.

But we *are* Men, close cousins to the monkeys, and we did leave the surface of Earth, and that is how I came to be drinking in Susie's Bar and Grill in Port Forlorn, on Lorn, most dismal of the Rim Worlds, that night, and that is how Halvorsen came to find me there.

I'll say this for Halvorsen; he didn't look like a monkey's cousin. He looked like a monkey. He didn't need to put his hands over his eyes or his ears or his mouth to look like one of the three wise monkeys, however. He looked like a smallish, grey ape that has lived long enough to achieve and, even, to surpass human intelligence. He was skinny, but carried a pronounced pot belly. His dark, wizened face was framed by bushy grey side whiskers, and from it stared two large, mournful, brown eyes.

I felt those eyes staring at me. I felt them for seconds before I lifted my head from my arms and looked into them, across the table with its filled-to-overflowing ashtrays, its dirty glasses, its little, stagnant pools of spilled drinks.

I was in no mood for company. That was why my friends – second and third mates of the *Rimhoud*, their girls and my girl – had left me. I was feeling disgusted with everything and everybody, including myself, and the more that I drank the more disgusted I was feeling.

'Go away,' I said to Halvorsen. 'Go away. I don't know what you're selling, but I don't want any today, thank you. Not today. Not ever.'

'How do you know?' he countered.

'Because I know everything,' I replied. 'Liquor makes me that way. I know that the Universe is just a cesspit and the stars and planets no more than ordure ...'

He said, 'I want to know everything.'

'I've told you everything there is to know,' I said.

He smiled sadly, pulled out a chair and sat down. He lifted a hand in oddly imperious gesture. Susie herself waddled over to our table, took his order. She returned with a bottle of imported whisky – not the real Scotch, but that distilled on Nova Caledon is close enough – and a couple of clean glasses, set them down before us and smiled fatly. She treated the little monkey, as I was regarding him, with a deference that I found annoying.

Halvorsen poured each of us a drink. He raised his glass and said, 'To the key ...' He drank, and I drank.

'What key?' I asked.

'The key that I am looking for,' he replied.

'I haven't got it,' I said.

'You can help me to find it,' he told me.

'What the hell is all this about?' I demanded.

He said, making a statement rather than asking a question, 'You're Charles Merrill, aren't you?'

'Yes,' I admitted.

'You hold a Master Astronaut's Certificate of Competency. You were, until recently, Second Officer of the *Rimbird*. Prior to that you were with the Trans-Galactic Clippers ...'

'So,' I cracked brilliantly, 'what?'

'So I need a Master Astronaut. I'm willing to pay handsomely for your services.'

'Listen,' I said, 'I've had Space. I've had Space in a big way. I'm sick of tank-grown food and recirculated air and water. When I paid off from the *Rimbird* I swore that I'd never set foot in a spaceship again, and I meant it.'

'Times have changed since then,' he remarked. 'You paid off from the *Rimbird* to get married, to find yourself a shore job. But the girl didn't marry you, and so you never got that sinecure in her father's business. You're polishing an office stool with the seat of your pants and hating it. You come in here every Friday night to get a load on and to swap stories with your old shipmates.'

It was true, but nobody likes being told the truth. I was tempted to let him have what remained in my glass full in the face, but thought better of it. Fat Susie was watching us, and Susie, for some reason, had always been willing to give me credit. Susie, I had observed over the past few months, deplored rowdiness in her establishment and did her utmost to discourage it. I decided that I did not want to get in Susie's bad books.

'And who the hell are *you*, anyhow?' I asked him.

'My name is Halvorsen,' he said quietly.

'Never heard of you,' I grunted. 'Not that I particularly want to.'

He smiled, and looked more like a sad little monkey than ever. 'Such is fame,' he sighed. 'You must have seen my name every day of your life, Mr Merrill – aboard your ships, on every civilised planet.'

'Sorry,' I said insicerely, 'it rings no bell.' I got to my

feet. 'Excuse me. I want to shake hands with an old friend.'

Halvorsen looked at me inquiringly when I came back.

'So,' I sneered as I sat down, 'you're *that* Halvorsen. Halvorsen, the Outhouse King, sitting on his throne of vitrified porcelain ...'

He flushed. He said, 'I'm a rich man, Mr Merrill, but how I made my money is of no importance, except that it was made honestly. I'm a rich man, and I pay well. At the moment, I need a yacht-master. Levin, who was my captain, got himself knocked down by a ground car on the day after we arrived here and will be in hospital for months yet.'

'I've had Space,' I told him again, 'in a big way. In any case, I've no desire to become a hired hand, a ... a *flunkey*.'

'If you take the job,' he assured me, 'you'll be no more a flunkey than my secretary, or my physician.'

'You can call me Admiral,' I said, 'with pay and uniform to match, and I'll still not be interested. Take my tip and go to see old Grimes, the Astronautical Superintendent of Rim Runners. He may be able to loan you an officer.'

'I've already seen Commodore Grimes,' said Halvorsen. 'He told me that he's very short of officers at the moment, and that all his officers are under contract and can't be released. He told me about you, and the places where I'd be likely to find you on a Friday night.'

'So he told you about me,' I growled. 'What did he tell you? 'One of our most promising young officers, who threw away his career for a floosie?' Or did he say that I was a no-hoper and no loss to Rim Runners?'

'He said,' replied Halvorsen, 'that you were a good man gone wrong, and that you were in crying need of rehabilitation.'

'You can take your rehabilitation,' I started to say, 'and ...'

It was the look of contempt in the girl's eyes that stopped me. She had come in without my noticing her and was now standing behind Halvorsen. If he was a monkey, she was a cat. She had the slim sleekness of the well-bred Siamese and something of the same colouring, and her blue eyes held only feline disdain. *Who is this drunken bum?* She seemed to ask, although her wide, scarlet mouth did not move.

Halvorsen saw me staring at her, half-turned in his chair.

'Leona,' he said, his face lighting up. He sprang to his feet. Clumsily, unwillingly, I followed suit. 'Mr Merrill, I'd like you to meet my secretary, Miss Leona Wayne. Leona, this is Mr Merrill, whom I hope to persuade to take Captain Levin's place.'

She acknowledged the introduction and heard the news without enthusiasm.

'*Starmaid* runs herself, Mr Halvorsen,' she stated coldly. 'Even I can handle her.'

'Can you handle an emergency?' I asked her.

'Can *you*?' she countered.

'That's my job,' I said.

Halvorsen bustled off and brought back a chair from another table. He fussed around Leona as she sat down. I resumed my own seat. All the time the girl's cold eyes were fixed on mine. Already I was beginning to hate her – the coolness of her, the sleekness, the plain, expensive clothing that achieved effect by cut rather than by ornamentation, the slender elegance of the body that was its foundation.

'I've heard about these ships that run themselves,' I said. 'Lloyd's of London won't touch them with a barge pole, and Federation astronautical law insists that at least one Master Astronaut be carried lest they become a menace to decent commercial shipping.'

'One needn't insure with Lloyd's, she said. 'We don't deal with them.'

'You still have to observe Federation law,' I told her. 'Even here. Even on the Rim.'

'A pity,' she said.

'How soon can you join?' asked Halvorsen, breaking into the *tête-à-tête*.

'I haven't said that I am joining,' I said.

'Don't press him,' said the girl.

'I should give a month's notice to my present employers,' I said.

'I,' Halvorsen assured me, 'am not without influence. Can you join tonight? We can get your name on the Register tomorrow.'

'What's the job worth?' I asked, hoping to deepen the expression of disgust on the girl's face. My hope was realised.

Halvorsen told me. He named a figure that would have made the master of an Alpha-class liner envious. He promised free transportation, First Class, to any part of the Galaxy on the termination of my employment and my reinstatement, if I so desired, in T.-G. Clippers. More for the hell of it than anything else I pressed for a uniform allowance over and above my handsome salary. Halvorsen did not quibble. His secretary looked as though she would be paying for everything out of her own pocket.

We left Susie's Bar and Grill shortly thereafter. Big, fat Susie bowed us to the door, treating Halvorsen as though he were royalty – as, in a sense, he was. Did not every human and humanoid in the Galaxy pay him tribute at least once daily? There was a chauffeur-driven hired car waiting outside, its gyroscope humming softly. The driver opened the door of the passenger cabin with a flourish. Leona Wayne climbed first into the monowheel; I stood back to let Halvorsen follow her, but he urged me to take precedence. I sat down beside the girl. She edged away from me. At once I was acutely conscious of my shabby clothing, my long unpolished shoes, the fact that I had let three days go by without using depilatory cream.

Halvorsen seated himself on the other side of me.

'Where to, Mr Halvorsen?' asked the driver.

'The spaceport,' answered my new employer.

We skimmed through the narrow streets of the Pleasure Quarter, through the bright, meretricious glare of neon signs, through the waves of trite, tawdry music that billowed out through the open doors of bars and night clubs. Then we were among the warehouses, black cliffs that towered up, on either hand, to the black sky. The few sparse lights served only to accentuate their blackness, as did the faint, far nebulosities in the empty, Rim World firmament, glimpsed now and again from the bottom of our man-made canyon. Old newspapers, driving before the omnipresent bitter wind, gleamed in the beam of our headlamp like soiled, white birds. Ahead of us, growing brighter, was the harsh brilliance of working lights, the spaceport.

We swept through the gate after only cursory formalities. We passed the gleaming tower that was *Rimhound*, loading for Ultimo, Thule and Faraway. We rolled past the berth in which *Rimbird* was discharging the merchandise she had loaded on the Eastern Circuit – Stree, Mellise, Tharn and Grollor. We left behind us the whining, snarling machinery, the busy conveyor belts, cranes and gantries. We ran out to an almost unused corner of the field, threading our way through and among towering piles of junk.

My first impression of *Starmaid* was of smallness. She was dwarfed by an upended tube liner – one of those from the Trans-Galactic Clipper *Thermopylae*, left at Port Forlorn after she had put in for repairs – was hardly bigger than an almost porous propellant tank discarded from some other ship.

My second impression was of cleanliness and of neatness. *Starmaid* would have looked neat and clean in any surroundings, but she lost nothing by contrast with the interstellar junk with which she was surrounded. I realised that I had lived for too long without love, and that this little ship would do much to fill the emotional vacuum.

We got out of the car, stepped down to the dirty, scarred concrete. Halvorsen walked briskly to the airlock door, fussed with the combination lock. There was about him the air, outrageously incongruous, of the suburban householder returning home after a party. He got the door open, stood to one side. Leona Wayne went to enter, but he put out a restraining hand.

He said, 'This is only a little ship, but I like to observe naval etiquette. The Master takes precedence over the Purser when boarding.'

'And over the Owner?' I asked.

'Over the bio-chemist,' he replied. 'There are no idlers aboard *Starmaid*. After you, Captain Merrill.'

'Thank you,' I replied.

I walked first into the little airlock, hardly larger than a telephone booth, ignoring the venomous glance that Leona Wayne shot in my direction. Once inside the ship I insisted that Halvorsen take the lead – after all, he knew his way around; I didn't. The drive had sobered me up and I was able to take an intelligent interest in all that I saw.

She was more than just a little ship. She was a big ship – and a big ship of the better class, at that – in miniature. She had everything, including gear that was still too expensive to be built into the T.-G. Clippers of the

Commission's liners. There was, for example, a set of remote controls so that the Mannschenn Drive unit could be operated from the Reaction engine room, and another allowing the rockets to be controlled from the Interstellar Drive compartment. (This, however, was necessary, since *Starmaid* carried only one engineer, he being qualified to take charge of both propulsive systems.) The galley, Leona Wayne's domain (she was Catering Officer as well as Purser) was a gleaming miracle of automation. There was automatic monitoring for the yeast and tissue culture vats and the hydroponics tanks – but this, Halvorsen confessed, was usually disconnected as he enjoyed pottering.

We went up to the Control Room before we inspected the accommodation. This was in keeping with the rest of the ship. There were such luxuries as Mass Proximity Indicators, usually only found in the Survey Fleet. There was a Mark VII Geigenheim Electronic Navigator – and this, I knew, would be capable of taking *Starmaid* from one side of the Galaxy to the other. I resolved to do the same as Halvorsen had done with his electronic monitors. The Geigenheim made the ship intelligent – but she still had no imagination, and it is imagination alone that keeps Man superior to the thinking machines of his own making. It wasn't all mechanical.

We looked into the Radio Office. I was rather surprised to see that there was no dividing line drawn between electronic and psionic radio – the dog's brain amplifier was out of place among the severely utilitarian transceivers and radar gear. Halvorsen explained that there had been more doubling up, that his Communications Officer was one of those rare people who, in addition to their telepathic talents, have the ability to comprehend and to cope with electronic equipment. It was clear that nothing but the best was good enough for my new employer. I began to feel acutely conscious of my own shortcomings and began to wonder what was the urgency, whey he could not wait for the recovery of Captain Levin who, to judge by the standards of his shipmates, must have been an outstanding astronaut.

I raised the point a little later when the three of us were sitting in the small, beautifully furnished saloon, drinking the excellent coffee that Leona had made.

'I'm an old man, Captain Merrill,' said Halvorsen. 'I'm an old man and beginning to get impatient. There's so much that I want to know before I go . . .'

'Is it that key you're looking for?' I asked.

'Yes. I'm looking for the key. I want to find out, if I can, if there's any meaning to the Universe, any meaning to life. I've already spent a fortune hiring out other men's brains; they've come up with all sorts of fancy variations of the Unified Field Theory, but not one of them makes any real sense . . .'

'The Halvorsen Foundation . . .' I said. 'I should have remembered.'

'Yes. The Halvorsen Foundation, set up to discover what we are, *why* we are. I'm tired of waiting for the scientists to cook up any sort of intelligible answer and so I decided to find out for myself. I thought that I might find the key out here on the Rim, out here where our expanding, exploding Galaxy is pressing against the ultimate nothingness . . .'

'But what *are* you looking for?' I asked.

He hesitated before replying. He asked, 'Are you a religious man?'

'No,' I said truthfully.

'Then you have an open mind, presumably. I hope so – although I have found atheists to be as savagely intolerant as deists. But if you're an agnostic . . .'

'I am,' I interrupted.

'Good. I've become rather hesitant about mentioning my current line of research before strangers. The deists accuse me of blasphemy, of impious prying into secrets that were never meant to be revealed; the atheists accuse me of trying to bolster up archaic superstitions. Be that as it may, what I'm investigating is the continuous creation of matter. It was Hoyle, a twentieth-century astronomer, who first stumbled on to it, who put forward the theory that there was a continual influx of new hydrogen atoms into the Universe from ... from *somewhere*. Hydrogen atoms, the very building blocks of all matter. The theory was never disproved and in Hoyle's time, when the average scientist tended to be something of a mystic, was quite widely accepted. But mysticism is frowned upon now and Hoyle's theory of continuous creation has been explained away. The Galaxy is expanding, they tell us, and as all Space is filled with hydrogen atoms it is only natural that there should be an apparent influx.

'That explanation never satisfied me. I had *Starmaid* built to my own specifications, recruited her crew. I brought her out to the Rim. I ran out past the Rim, beyond the Rim – fifty light years, a hundred, two hundred, a thousand ...'

'It seemed like a thousand years,' said the girl. 'Years, not light years... They complain of the cold and the dark on these Rim Worlds; they don't know what the words mean.'

'There was emptiness,' said Halvorsen, 'an emptiness far beyond anything found in interstellar space. I doubt if there was one atom to a million cubic miles, and my Mass Proximity Indicator is fantastically sensitive. It was obvious that the hydrogen atoms aren't being swept in from Outside, equally obvious that this continuous creation is a phenomenon confined to the Galaxy – and, it could be, to the other galaxies ...'

'What do you hope to find?' I asked. 'And where do you hope to find it?'

'There is one answer to both questions,' he said. 'I

don't know. But I have heard of the philosophical lizards of Stree, and it may be that they will be able to give me some clue. I want to leave for Stree tomorrow.'

'Tomorrow?'

'The ship is fully stored and bunkered, Captain Merrill,' said the girl. 'All that is required is the legal formality of placing your name on the Register. If you've forgotten all you ever knew of pilotage and navigation it doesn't matter; as I've told you, the ship can handle herself if need be.'

'I've not forgotten,' I said sharply. I turned to Halvorsen. 'There are things that have to be checked, sir. There are my own personal affairs to wind up . . .'

'You can be ready by tomorrow evening,' he told me.

'*This* evening,' said Leona Wayne, looking at her watch.

'This evening,' amended Halvorsen.

I was.

I was ready, and *Starmaid* was ready, and we lifted from Port Forlorn at precisely 1900 hours, Local Time. It had been a rush getting all secured for Space. There were the legal formalities – and didn't somebody once remark that the tide runs sluggishly through official channels? There were my own private affairs to be clewed up, and there was the thorough inspection of the ship and all her gear that I insisted upon before I would take over.

The most important event of the day, I think, was the visit to Captain Levin in the Port Forlorn hospital. He was not the man that I had expected to find; I had visualised somebody much older, somebody with the manner and appearance of a senior master in the Trans-Galactic Clippers or the Interstellar Transport Commission. He was a young man, hardly older than myself. He was frankly envious of me, and he was willing to talk.

'They're a good crowd,' he told me. 'Leona's only fault

is her damned snootiness, her refusal to make allowances for human frailties. But she's a good cook and a good purser, and she can navigate as well as you or I. The Old Boy's harmless enough – and I'd always be willing to sign him on as biochemist if he lost his fortune and had to work for a living again. Doc Rayner is pretty harmless – the only trouble with *him* is that he's too engrossed in keeping Halvorsen alive and kicking to worry much about us lesser mortals. He's a geriatrician, of course, one of *the* geriatricians, so anybody on the sunny side of seventy isn't of much interest to him. Then there's Cressy. If he isn't thinking about electronics he's thinking about psionics, and if he isn't thinking about either he's thinking about both. Leave him to his printed circuits and his dog's brain in aspic and he's quite happy. MacIlwraith can be hard to get on with. He's one of those engineers with the odd idea that the ship exists only to house her precious machinery. He'll always do what you want, though, even if he's apt to run screaming to Halvorsen about it afterwards ...'

I met them all during the day. Rayner looked as though he himself were in crying need of the services of a geriatrician. He looked older than his patient, was no more than a perambulatory assemblage of brittle bones held together by dried skin and sinew. Cressy was only a youngster – the sort of youngster who wears pebble-lensed spectacles and has become a junior chess champion long before the onset of puberty. MacIlwraith was a hulking, carrot-topped brute who must have had Neanderthalers in his ancestry. He made it clear to me from the start that I was only a Control Room ornament and inessential to the real work of the ship. He took orders, however, albeit grudgingly. He would have been far happier if those orders had come directly from the owner and not from a mere master, such as I represented.

This, then, was my crew. This was the crew of the

sweet, shining *Starmaid*. This was the little company that was dedicated to the search for ... for *something* in the realms of the eternal *nothing*. I was dedicated to the same search, even though I knew that it was crazy. A man will do a lot for money. A man will do a lot - let us admit it - for the chance to get back into Space again.

At 1900 hours we lifted. At 1845 I was siting in my acceleration chair in Control, looking out through the wide viewports. There was little to see - a chill drizzle had swept down from the hills to enshroud Port Forlorn. Dimly I could make out the glare of the working lights around *Rimbird* and *Rimhound*, the fainter glow of the city a little beyond them. Overhead the sky was overcast.

Halvorsen was in the special chair that he had caused to be installed in *Stairmaid*'s control room - it was well to one side and out of the way. Leona Wayne was sitting in the navigator's chair. This was the first ship in which I had served in which the purser was interested in navigation; but there has to be, I told myself, a first time for anything.

She handled the pre-blast-off exchanges with the Control Tower competently enough, made the routine checks without hesitation. I could not fault her counting down.

'Zero!' she said at last.

Starmaid lifted, obedient to my fingers on the controls. She lifted, and the glare of her exhaust was reflected from the clouds through which we drove. She lifted, but slowly - I was remembering the old, brittle bones of Halvorsen, my employer, the old, brittle bones of Rayner, the surgeon. Too, *Starmaid* was not a commercial ship; there was no need for me to conserve reaction mass by getting upstairs in as big a hurry as the structural members would stand. She lifted, and with every mile of gained altitude I was getting the feel of her. By the time that we were clear of the overcast I was beginning to think that I was her Master in fact as well as in name.

Halvorsen smiled at me, saying, 'She's a sweet little ship.'

'I'm finding that out,' I replied.

'She is also,' remarked Leona Wayne coldly, 'a tough ship. She doesn't need to be babied.'

I swallowed the hot retort, returning my attention to the instruments. If there had to be ill feeling, I would not be its initiator. I made sure that the needle of the accelerometer stayed steadily on the Half G graduation, affected a great show of interest in the skin temperature gauges. I was conscious all the time of the girl's cold eyes on my every action. I wondered if my predecessor had had to put up with this tacit back-seat driving.

Lorn was no more than a great, misty ball below us. Ahead was the blackness, with the sparse pinpoints of light that were stars, of Outer Space; out to starboard was the glowing lens of the Galaxy. I cut the Drive, letting *Starmaid's* momentum carry her up and out. I actuated the gyroscopes, watched the cartwheel sight in the very nose of the ship swing slowly towards the glowing, orange speck that was the sun around which Stree revolved.

Dimly I was aware of a slender hand holding a sheet of paper before my nose. Irritated, I snapped, 'What is it?'

'The coordinates of our trajectory,' replied Leona Wayne. 'I fed the data into the Geigenheim while you were so busy piloting.'

'Thanks,' I said, 'but I'll not be needing the Geigenheim for this run. It's no more than the shortest distance between two points with nothing in the way . . .'

'How do you know there's not?' she demanded.

'Miss Wayne,' I growled, 'I've been on the Eastern

Circuit for over eighteen months. There's not so much as a swarm of micro-meteorites between Lorn and Stree.'

I juggled with the gyroscope controls, put the orange star in the exact centre of the sights, held it there. I sounded the acceleration alarm, fired all tubes. I let the speed build up gradually, never exceeding one gravity acceleration. Lorn was well astern when I cut the rockets and ordered the Mannschenn Drive started.

The journey from Lorn to Stree is not a long one, in terms of subjective time – the direct journey, that is; it's long enough when you have stoppages for loading and discharge on Tharn, Grollor and Mellise, with the consequent detours. It wasn't a long voyage for *Starmaid*. It was hardly long enough for me to get to know my new shipmates properly – and *Starmaid* was a ship in which all hands tended to do their own jobs quietly and efficiently with little inclination for social intercourse.

When he was not busy with his not very onerous duties as biochemist old Halvorsen shut himself in his cabin, studying the tapes that he had bought on Lorn concerning Stree. MacIlwraith, the engineer, lived for and with his smoothly functioning machinery. Cressy spent all his time telepathically nattering with his colleagues in other ships and shore stations throughout the Galaxy. Old Dr Rayner had little enough to do, but he sought nobody's company and seemed happy enough cataloguing his stamp collection.

Then, of course, there was Leona. Her hobby – if hobby it could be called – was the pursuit and the destruction of dirt. Her galley was spotless, as were here storerooms. Her little office was almost impossibly tidy. The small public rooms gleamed from deck to deckhead. With this I had no fault to find – but when, one day, I came into the Control Room to make a routine check of her position and found her dusting and polishing I decided that it was time to draw a line.

'Please,' I said, 'leave the Control Room alone.' I pulled myself across to the navigator's desk, which had been cleared of all books and papers. 'Where is my work book? Where are the tables and the ephemera?'

'In the drawers where they belong,' she replied shortly.

'Miss Wayne,' I told her, 'I appreciate what you've done in here. Really I do,' I went on, lying diplomatically. 'But I'm an untidy man, and I know it, and I have my own filing system. When things are left *my* way I can find anything I want in a split micro-second. Now ...'

'And now you can't, I suppose!' she flared. 'Captain Merrill, I don't see how you can live and work in such filth!'

'Filth?' I asked mildly. 'Isn't that rather a strong word? Absurdly strong? After all, there's clean dirt and dirty dirt, and a slight untidiness can hardly be classed as either ...'

'A slight untidiness? And what about the cigarette ash over everything? What about that?'

'It does no harm. It has occurred to me, though, that our employer could devote his time and his genius to inventing a really efficient Free Fall ashtray ...'

'So now,' she accused me, 'you're sneering at Mr Halvorsen, the man who picked you off the beach and gave you a job ...'

'I had a job at the time,' I reminded her. 'I have nothing against Mr Halvorsen – but, after all, I was doing him the favour, not the other way round.'

'That,' she said, 'doesn't give you the right to turn this ship into a pigsty.'

'Get this straight,' I told her, 'the only person in a ship in Deep Space who has any rights is the Master – even the Master of a yacht, even when the owner's aboard. The Master has the right to keep his Control Room in whatever condition of untidiness he pleases. I am exercising that right now. Will you please leave, Miss Wayne, and take your polishing rags with you?'

I didn't think that it was an excessively harsh reprimand – after all, I'd often heard far harsher ones delivered by irate masters to female members of their crews. After all, when women come into Deep Space, with the rank and pay of spacemen, they must expect to take the rough with the smooth. I was rather congratulating myself for not having flown off the handle properly, was pulling books and papers from the drawers and sliding them under the elastic webbing of the table in my usual untidy manner, when I heard a sniffing sound.

I looked around. I was surprised and shocked to see that Leona Wayne, the icily calm, efficient Miss Wayne, was sobbing.

Damn it all, I thought, she's the purser. She can't expect to be handled as though she's labelled *Fragile* top, sides and bottom. She's trodden on my corns, and she's had her corns trodden on in return, and so what?

'Miss Wayne,' I heard myself saying, 'if I said anything to upset you, I apolgise . . .'

'It's not what you've said, you stupid brute!' she wailed. 'It's what you've done. This was such a nice, clean, *tidy* ship before you came here. And now . . .'

Somehow, I was holding her, and she was sniffling damply between my neck and my shoulder. I remembered what little I had seen of Levin, the slight aura of effeminacy that had hung around him – not that he was any worse as a spaceman for that. I thought of the old-maidish MacIlwraith and the equally old-maidish Rayner – and, come to that, old Halvorsen had a certain prissiness about him . . . And there was Cressy, with his love of gossip – even if it was intra-Galactic gossip . . . And when I joined the ship I had sensed, subconsciously, that all those in her were house-proud rather than ship-proud. (And yet Leona had taken care to impress upon me that *Starmaid* was a tough ship ...)

So she didn't like dirt and untidiness, and she had shipped away in a yacht full of fussy, old-maidish bachelors, and then I'd come, with my slovenly habits, and had assumed the role of the proverbial bull in the china shop, the serpent in a hitherto gleaming and spotless Eden. It was just too bad, and I had no intention of promising to mend my ways. (I might try to mend them, but that would depend to a large extent upon the outcome of events. I raised her tear-stained face and I kissed her, and thought that I might, perhaps, try to keep my desk a little tidier and dispose of my cigarette ash in the receptacles provided ...)

She said, 'But you must remember, Charles, you must try to remember how much I hate dirt and untidiness. Its almost a phobia with me. That's why I agreed to come away in this yacht when all the other secretaries, senior to me, had turned the chance down. Space is so *clean* ...'

I said that I'd try to remember – and it wasn't a case of anything for a quiet life either. I had realised suddenly that I'd wanted the girl ever since my first sight of her.

The others accepted the situation philosophically enough. I was half afraid that there would be jealousies and resentments, but I need not have worried on that score. I don't think that any of them was interested, even. Each had his own interests, and sex was not among them. His engines were MacIlwraith's shining mistresses, and so long as Cressy could indulge in his neighbourly, back-fence gossip with other telepaths, *he* was happy. The doctor had his stamp collection, and the only female in old Halvorsen's life was that naked Truth who, in the old legends, was alleged to live at the bottom of a well.

(And how close to the actuality those old legends were, we had no idea!)

As for me – I was lucky, and I knew it. I had a ship and I had a woman, and what more can a man ask? True, the woman was over-insistent upon cleanliness and tidiness, but that was a small fault. I could endure that for the sake of all the rest. And after all – until men are capable of building the perfect ship what right have they to expect the perfect woman?

And so, as the subjective days passed, we fell towards Stree. Both Leona and I were sorry when my observations showed me that it was time to return to the normal continuum, time to throw ourselves into an orbit around the planet and to manoeuvre the ship into her landing spiral.

But there was Stree below us – an ochreous ball, mainly barren rock and desert. There were the signals coming in, loud and clear, from the beacon at Port Grimes. There was the sibilant voice of Stressor, the Rim Runners' agent, saying, '*Starmaid*, your request received. You may land.'

We came in, dropping through the clear, arid atmosphere, dropping down to the expanse of arid sand that was the spaceport. We came in, with *Starmaid* obedient to my hand on the controls, with Leona sitting at my side and refraining, now, from back-seat driving, with old Halvorsen beaming at us like a benevolent, wise old monkey. We came in slowly, balancing atop the pillar of fire that was our interplanetary drive, falling gently to the circle of fused slag that showed where the backblasts of *Faraway Quest*, of *Lorn Lady*, of *Rimbird*, *Rimhound*, *Rimfire* and *Jolly Swagman* had splashed over the surface.

We landed gently, softly. I cut the drive, pressed the switch that would make the *Finished with Engines* signal in the engine room.

'We're here.' I said, unnecessarily.

I looked through the viewport. I saw Stressor hurrying

out of the Port Master's office, looking, from this distance, like one of the dinosaurs that were once the dominant life form on at least a thousand worlds, that would still be the dominant life form if they had learned to adapt themselves, as had Stressor's ancestors.

'What – I mean *who* – is that?' asked Halvorsen.

'That's Stressor,' I said. 'You heard his voice on the R/T when he asked permission to land. He's Rim Runners' local agent.'

'You're familiar with these people, Captain Merrill,' said Halvorsen. 'I'll leave you to do the honours.'

'As you please, Mr Halvorsen,' I replied. Then, to Leona: 'You'd better put the kettle on. The Streen love a friendly chat over the teacups.'

I went down to the airlock. Stressor was surprised to see me. He clasped my hand in both of his, the rough scales bruising my skin.

'Mr Merrill – or should I say Captain Merrill? This is indeed a pleasure! I was told that you had left the service.'

'I had,' I said. 'But I came back. Welcome aboard, Stressor. Will you join us for tea?'

'You are gracious.'

He got through our little airlock with some difficulty, followed me up to the saloon. I introduced him to Halvorsen, and then to Leona who came in from the pantry with the tea things. I told him that *Starmaid* was not a trading vessel, and he found the concept of a private yacht rather difficult to grasp.

'But,' he said, 'you must have come here for *something*.'

'We did,' averred Halvorsen. 'Knowledge.'

'Knowledge?' This was something that a native of Stree could understand. 'Then you have come to the right world, Mr Halvorsen. Knowledge is the one commodity in which we are rich.'

'Then you can help me?' asked Halvorsen.

'What knowledge do you want?' asked the native.

'There must be some ... some key to the secret of the Universe,' said Halvorsen. 'Have you got it?'

Stressor delicately sipped his tea, the cup looking tiny and fragile in his talons, against his gaping, needle-toothed mouth. He said, 'There is a key; we have known that for generations. We have discussed it for as many generations. Some of our philosophers say that they know what it is, say that what they have learned of human customs since our first contact with your race has given them the answer. There are those of us who cannot accept that answer, myself among them. We are not, as Captain Merrill will tell you, an overly proud people – but even humility has its limits ...'

Halvorsen's eyes were shining.

'What *is* the key?' he demanded.

'Sir,' Stressor replied siffly, 'I will not tell you. I, like you, am an intelligent being, and feel that this universe was crated so that intelligent beings might appreciate it, come to a full understanding of it. All I can suggest is that you see Ossan. He is too old to have much pride left ...'

'Can you bring him here?' asked Halvorsen.

'He is too old to travel,' said Stressor.

As Stressor had told us, the Streen are not an overly proud people. They consider it no disgrace to act as beasts of burden. So it was that the following day, early, Halvorsen, Leona and myself, riding in saddles strapped to the backs of three of the Streen, set out for the rugged, hilly country in which Ossan lived. Stressor came with us, laden with gifts for the ancient philosopher as well as with our own food supplies, leading what could, incorrectly, be called the cavalcade. The mode of transport was not too uncomfortable – but it is rather disconcerting to be expected to carry on a conversation with the animal you are riding . . .

It was late afternoon when we reached the cave in which Ossan lived – a dark hole in a sheer cliff of red sandstone. He came shambling into the sunlight, blinking his filmed eyes. The scales of his body were flaking, crumbling almost, and the dry, musty stench of him was overpowering. He said something that was all clicks and hisses. Stressor replied in kind.

My mount turned his great, reptilian head on the long neck and said, 'You can get down, Captain Merrill. Ossan has said that he will talk to you.'

We got down, glad enough of the chance to stretch our legs. We took advantage of the slight breeze and stood to windward of the aged Streen, watched while Stressor displayed the gifts that we had brought – the tea, the sugar, the books. Halvorsen looked disappointed when the lizard philosopher displayed no great interest in the latter. The hissing, clicking conversation continued.

Stressor at last translated.

'Ossan says,' he told us, 'that first of all you must tell him all about yourselves – who you are, what you are, what you have seen. He says that you Earthmen brought the idea of trade to this world, and that he will trade knowledge for knowledge, ideas for ideas.'

So we spread our sleeping bags – they had been carried in Stressor's pack – on the hard rock and sat down. Halvorsen talked first, with lengthy pauses for translation. He told of his humble youth as a plumber, of the invention of the first really satisfactory Free Fall toilet that had brought him fame – and to have one's name spread throughout the Galaxy in every ship is fame – and fortune. He talked of the intricacies of finance, of the problems of manufacture. He talked of the foundation that bore his name and that had yet to make any real contribution to the knowledge of mankind.

It was my turn next. I talked of the worlds I had seen, of

the people I had met, of life in the starships. Had Leona not been there I might have talked of the women I had known.

When Leona told her story it was dark, and the few, faint stars were shining in the black sky. It was dark, and it was cold, and Stressor broke out the efficient little heater from his pack and set it up so that we all derived some benefit from the warmth. He made tea, too, and we sipped the hot fluid gratefully. After he had finished his cup the old philosopher hissed a few words to the agent, turned and vanished into his cave.

'He,' said Stressor, 'will talk in the morning.'

After a not very satisfying supper we crawled into our bags and tried to sleep, both Leona and myself resenting the presence of our employer and the great lizards.

Morning came, the sun striking our faces like a blow.

For a long, hazy moment I was completely bewildered, thought that I was recovering from the night's debauch, sleeping in some gutter in Port Forlorn. I opened my eyes and saw the red cliffs, the clear sky. I saw Leona emerging from the cocoon of her sleeping bag, still neat and unruffled in spite of the primitive conditions in which we had slept. I saw Halvorsen stretching his arms and yawning, looking not like a wise old ape but, at this moment, like an exceptionally stupid one. I saw Stressor and the three Streen who had carried us, rising from the hollow in the rocks where, curled lizardlike, they had slept.

Leona went to our supply pack, got out cleansing tissues, comb and mirror, wandered a little way down the ravine to where a bend hid her from sight. While she was gone I busied myself with our portable stove, with water and tea, with self-heating cans of rations. The Streen watched with interest but no envy. Our food was unpalatable to them and, reptiles that they were, they could go for weeks without sustenance. Even so, they had become addicted to tea and when the boiling water was poured over the leaves their wide nostrils began to twitch.

Halvorsen got out of his bag and went along the ravine in the opposite direction to that taken by Leona. Stressor said, 'That is one thing we have in common with you Earthmen – a desire for privacy on certain occasions.' I didn't feel in a very philosophical mood, grunted a curt acknowledgement. I knew Stressor of old, knew that with very little encouragement he could deliver a long and boring lecture on sanitation as practised in various parts of the Galaxy, the bulk of the material garnered from the tapes and books that Rim Runners' ships had brought to this world.

There was a scrabbling noise inside the cave. Old Ossan emerged, looking more like a dinosaur that should have been extinct a million years ago than like one of the thinkers of his world.

He said simply, 'I smell tea.'

'But he can't speak English!' I exclaimed.

'He can,' said Stressor, 'when he wants to. This is one of the times.'

'Give me some tea,' demanded the ancient Streen.

I poured him a cup. He took it in his claws, drained it, almost boiling that it was. He held it to me to be refilled. He was gulping his third cup when Halvorsen and Leona returned.

'I am ready to talk,' he said. 'Listen carefully. You will not find what you search on the Rim. Your Key is not here. North you must run, and north again, north from the Centre. There, I think, you will find the Key. This I ask – that you let me know what it is that you find. I would know, before I die, if my theory is correct.'

'What is your theory?' asked Halvorsen.

Ossan was silent.

'We are a humble people,' said Stressor, 'but we have our pride. We hope that Ossan's theory is wrong. We hope that you will be able to prove that it is wrong.'

And that was all we could get out of any of them. There was some sort of taboo involved - but what it was we could not determine. Bribery was useless and we were in no position to make threats even if we had been so foolhardy as to ignore Federation law. So we said goodbye - without reluctance on the part of either Leona or myself - and let our carriers take us back to the ship.

Bitterly I resented Halvorsen's demon, the demon that was driving him so far and so fast in the pursuit of knowledge, the demon that was driving all of us so far and fast. Sun after sun we passed, world after world, planets that we had never seen before and might never have the chance to see again. The ship reeked of hot oil and metal and our combined body odours, efficient though her air conditioning system was. At no spaceport did we halt for more than the bare minimum of time necessary for us to replenish exhausted supplies. Had Halvorsen not been a heavy smoker I doubt that we should have halted at all - for all essentials *Starmaid* was a self-contained, self-perpetuating unit.

It should have been a honeymoon voyage for Leona and myself, but it was not. We, like the ship, like all in her, were too hard driven. Our tempers became frayed and we began to snap at each other. I forgot to maintain the standards of neatness upon which Leona had always insisted, and that made matters worse, so much so that my lapses became deliberate instead of accidental.

And so we drove on, across the Galaxy, across the northern 'surface' of the great Lens. We landed at last on Polaria, a world as bleak and desolate as any of the Rim Worlds, a world whose sparsely settled Northern Hemisphere looked always to the Ultimate Night. But it was not the emptiness of the sky that made that hemisphere unpopular – because the night sky was far from empty. It was alive with flowing, coalescing shapes, with great curtains and streamers of cold flame. It was beautiful – and frightening. It was something to marvel at, to admire – but not to live with. It was something to be explained scientifically that, in spite of the scientific explanations, still evoked a feeling of superstitious terror.

We made our landing in the north, although there was no spaceport there. We set *Starmaid* down on a great, level field of ice, staying her off against the perpetual bitter winds. We helped Halvorsen and Cressy to set up their instruments outside the ship, instruments that were, to me, a complete enigma. We watched MacIlwraith doing inexplicable things to his Mannschenn Drive unit. We left the specialists to their mysteries, went to talk with the old doctor.

He said, 'I'm an old man, Merrill, and I thought that I had lost the capacity to be afraid of anything – but I'm scared. I'm a scientists of sorts, Merrill, and until now I've always thought that there should be no limit to Man's knowledge – but now I'm no longer sure of that ...'

'But what are they doing, Dr Rayner?' asked the girl. 'What are they doing?'

'Mr Halvorsen thinks,' replied the doctor, 'that this is one of the sources from which the continuously created hydrogen atoms flow into the Universe. He has set up meters to measure that flow.'

'I guessed that,' I said. 'But what is MacIlwraith doing to the Drive? I know that I'm only the Captain, but I think that I'm entitled to some word of explanation from the Chief Engineer.'

'I can only guess,' said the old man. 'I heard them talking about it some time ago, before you joined us.

Halvorsen reasoned that the influx of primal matter must be from some other dimension, and MacIlwraith believes that it will be possible to adjust the Drive so that *Starmaid* can stem the stream, follow it to its real source.'

'Interdimensional travel is impossible,' I said. 'Like Time Travel, it's just something that science fiction writers play with.'

The doctor bared his teeth in a ghastly grin. 'That's just what the twentieth-century rocketeers must have said about the Faster Than Light Drive. Me, I know MacIlwraith well enough to be scared.'

'And I'm scared,' said Leona, drawing closer to me.

'I'm not,' I declared, not too untruthfully. 'I'm annoyed, legally speaking, I'm the Lord and Master of this wagon, notwithstanding the fact that Mr Halvorsen is the owner, I resent being kept in the dark.'

'And what,' asked a fresh voice, 'do you intend doing about it, Captain Merrill?'

I turned abruptly, saw our employer's figure framed in the doorway. He was still wearing the synthefurs that had protected him from the cold while he worked outside, although he had removed the gloves and thrown back the hood. His face was glowing with colour. He looked almost a young man, far younger than Dr Rayner's ministrations could ever have made him.

'Mr Halvorsen,' I said, 'I demand an explanation. I am Master of this ship, and I have discovered that Mr MacIlwraith is doing something to the most important of her propulsive units that could not, so far as I can gather, be classed as routine overhaul. In my opinion, he is jeopardising the safety of the vessel.'

'Are you an engineer, Captain Merrill?'

'No – but the fact that I hold a master's certificate gives me a smattering of engineering knowledge.'

'A smattering ... Captain Merrill, you are under

contract. Your contract binds you to take the ship from Point A to Point B, as required by the owner. I am the Owner. Should you refuse to carry out my instructions I could, should I so desire, sue you for breach of contract.'

'I can resign,' I said.

'You can give a month's notice,' he told me. 'But until that month, as measured by the GMT chronometer, has expired, you are bound to carry out my instructions. Should you stage a one-man strike – then Miss Wayne can handle the ship.'

'I'm with Charles in this,' said Leona.

Halvorsen smiled. He said, 'I realise that the voyage here from Stree has been a great strain on all of us. I know that I, myself, feel that I have come so close to my objective that I will let nothing stand in my way.' The smile vanished from his face. '*Nothing*. But I'm asking you, Captain Merrill, I'm asking you, not commanding you, to take *Starmaid* up as soon as MacIlwraith finishes his modifications.'

'Where to?' I demanded. 'Where to? And, come to that, what are the modifications? I'm no scientist, no engineer, but I do know that the Mannschenn Drive shouldn't be monkeyed with.'

'Where to?' echoed Halvorsen. 'If I knew, Merrill, I'd feed the data into the Geigenheim and let *Starmaid* take herself there. But I don't know – and that's why I have to have a human captain at the controls. Of course, if you're scared . . .'

'Damn you!' I swore. 'I am scared, and I'd be a fool if I weren't. I've heard all the stories about what happens when the Drive gets out of kilter and I've believed some of 'em. But I'll never let it be said that I was too scared . . . to . . .'

'To follow where a mere, glorified plumber led?' asked Halvorsen.

'I was trying to put the idea into more diplomatic language,' I admitted. 'But what *is* MacIlwraith playing at? Tell me that.'

'The only engineering that I know about is sanitary engineering,' said Halvorsen. 'But I think that I can give you a rough idea. *The* principle of the Mannschenn Drive is precession, gyroscopic precession. Its gyroscopes precess at right angles to the three dimensions of Space, in Time. But Time is only one of an infinitude of dimensions. What if we could achieve precession through Fifth, or Sixth, or Seventh Dimensions? What if we could precess into that dimension from which the flow of hydrogen atoms emanates?'

'And you think that MacIlwraith can do it,' I asked.

'I'm sure that MacIlwraith can do it,' he stated.

'But *should* MacIlwraith do it?' asked old Rayner.

'Getting religious in your old age, Doc?' sneered Halvorsen.

'No, but ...'

'Even you can't keep me alive and kicking much longer,' said Halvorsen. 'And when I've found the Key I'll be willing to make my exit.

The engineer, accompanied by Cressy, pushed his way into the little cabin. He looked more like a Neanderthaler who has just despatched an enemy with a stone club than a scientist who has just solved a knotty problem - but his air of triumph was unmistakable.

'Take her up as soon as you like!' he cried. 'The job's finished! Take her up as soon as you like!'

I looked at Leona. Her face was pale, and I thought I saw her lips frame the word, *'Don't!'* But if she said anything it was lost in the triumphant uproar created by Halvorsen, MacIlwraith and Cressy.

I took her up, the glare of our exhaust reflected from the icefield and yet not as bright as the aurora in that northern sky. I took her up, through and past the curtains and the streamers of cold fire, of pallid fire and rosy fire and fire that flaunted a purple such as no emperor ever wore. I took her up into the emptiness, the blackness – and the skin temperature gauges told me that Space, in this region, was far from being a vacuum.

Leona sat at my side, saying nothing. A little away from us was Halvorsen, chuckling happily over that fantastically sensitive Mass Proximity Indicator. I looked at him with distaste, reminded of some unpleasant, grey little monkey engrossed in some trifle that has captured its curiosity. And MacIlwraith, I thought, he's another of the same breed, an apeman, an apeman with brains, but still with that monkey taint to his character ... I turned to look at Leona, and remembered the old proverb: Curiosity killed the cat. *If Halvorsen's curiosity kills* my *cat,* I thought, *I'll wring his blasted neck.*

'You're bucking the stream, Merrill,' shouted Halvorsen. 'You're doing fine!'

'And what do I do next?' I asked.

'Cut the reaction drive as soon as you're ready. Turn on the Mannschenn.'

Nothing can happen, I thought. Nothing can possibly happen. I don't believe that anything can happen.

I cut the drive, felt the upsurge against my seat belt as the pseudo-gravity of acceleration abruptly died.

'Mannschenn Drive ready?' I asked. 'Mannschenn Drive ready!' came MacIlwraith's reply over the intercom. 'Mannschenn Drive *on!*' I said, throwing the switch. I heard the familiar whine of the starting gyroscopes, felt the familiar giddiness and loss of orientation in Time as well as Space as the temporal field built up. I looked at the stern vision plate, expecting to see the great, starry field astern of us that was the Galaxy undergo its familiar transformation into a topologist's nightmare in glorious technicolour.

Instead, it ... vanished.

There was a gleaming whiteness ahead of us, around us . . .

Ahead of us . . .

This I'll say for myself, I had the presence of mind to refrain from using the rockets. The Mannschenn Drive was still running, and any alteration to the ship's mass while that system of cock-eyed gyroscopes is in operation can have results that are catastrophic. I refrained from using the rockets, relied on the control surfaces. They surely shouldn't have worked – the ship was in airless Space (or was she?) – but they did. We turned away from the gleaming wall with which collision was imminent, pushed on and . . . and up? But every schoolboy knows there is neither up nor down in Space.

'I'm turning her,' I said. 'I'm turning her. We're going back out the way we came in – but you'd better tell MacIlwraith to run the Drive in reverse.'

'Why?' asked Halvorsen – but he had not disputed my decision to turn.

'Because I don't want to be thrown back into the Galaxy as free, individual hydrogen atoms, that's why.'

'How do you know?'

'It's a guess, and I hope it's a good one . . .'

I struggled to keep the ship in the centre of the great, convoluted, white-gleaming tunnel, and, even so, managed briefly to wonder just what had happened. Had the dimensional shift resulted in a vast increase of size? It must have, but the mechanics of it I was content to leave to the physicists if they ever believed our story, if they ever heard it, even.

I heard Halvorsen babbling excitedly into the intercom, heard the engineer's replies. I became aware that the droning song of the gyroscopes had faded, had restarted again on a slightly different note. Then there was light ahead of us – not a sterile whiteness any more but the great field of Galaxy, twisted and distorted beyond recognition, shining with a myriad of colours – but still the Galaxy.

For all its fairness I knew now what it was, and Leona, my once fanatically cleanly Leona, knew what it was too. Her lips curled in the familiar expression of repugnance and then, quite suddenly, she started to sob. She said brokenly to Halvorsen, 'You've ruined everything, for everybody. How can any decent person live in this Universe after what you've found? How can we endure the . . . filth?' Her sobbing became hysterical.

Shocked, I stared at her. Already there was a coarsening of her fine features, a subtle slumping of the fine, taut lines of her body, a foreshadowing of the slattern within that she had, until now, so firmly repressed. *It doesn't matter*, I wanted to say. *It doesn't matter, Leona – you're still you and I'm still me, and we have each other.* But it would not have been true. I was still myself and would be able to fall back into my bad old ways without effort; Leona would never be her old self again, and both of us knew it.

'What does she mean, Merrill?' asked Halvorsen.

My hand hesitated over the switch that I hoped – or did I so hope? – that would bring us back to normal Space and Time, to the fair worlds that were the homes of men, to the worlds that once we had thought were fair, once upon a time, a long time ago. I thought, *But* I'm *not fussy*. I pulled the switch, mechanically set about shaping our trajectory for Polaria.

'What does she mean, Merrill?' asked Halvorsen again.

'You know,' I said curtly. 'You know. I've already told you once. I told you when I first met you, back in Port Forlorn. Remember? When you said that you wanted to know *everything*, and I said that I'd already told you everything there was to know . . .

'Halvorsen, the not-so-wise monkey,' I sneered. 'Halvorsen, the Outhouse King! You have found your Key, Halvorsen, haven't you?'

'The Outhouse Key!'

THE HUMANOID TOUCH

Jack Williamson
author of THE HUMANOIDS

More than thirty years ago Jack Williamson created one of the finest science fiction novels of all time – THE HUMANOIDS. In this new novel he returns to his classic subject: the final confrontation of man and machine. THE HUMANOID TOUCH is a new peak for a master of science fiction.

'Decades before the current headlines about automaton, computers and robots, Jack Williamson was examining the relationship between humankind and machines in his stories of the Humanoids. Now, in THE HUMANOID TOUCH, the Grand Master of Science Fiction carries that saga to its final, irresistible step. This is science fiction at its best: thoughtful, thought-provoking, and thoroughly engrossing.' *Ben Bova*

SCIENCE FICTION 0 7221 9195 2 £1.75